"You've already made up your mind?"

Cindy couldn't believe it. Had Clay really discounted everything she'd told him about that company? "You're buying it?" she asked incredulously.

"Yes. I've started negotiations. You see, what I plan—"

"Then what was tonight's meeting all about?" Cindy interrupted.

His mouth twisted in a grin. "You enjoyed it, didn't you?"

"That's not the point!" she snapped, her face burning at the thought of how thoroughly she *had* enjoyed the evening. "If you don't care what I think, if you have no regard for my professional opinion, why did you hire me?"

"Now, wait a minute. I always study your reports very carefully."

"And then do exactly what you please!"

"I think I do have that prerogative," he said wryly.

"Granted. You are the boss. But that doesn't give you the right to manipulate me! I'm not one of your—" Cindy broke off, more furious at herself than at him. She'd fallen into his arms as hungrily as one of those hungry women who haunted his office. . . .

Eva Rutland began writing when her four children, now all successful professionals, were growing up. She has become a regular—and very popular—contributor to Harlequin's Romance and Regency series. Readers of her first Romance, *To Love Them All*, will recognize Steve and Marcy Prescott, who play a secondary role in *No Accounting For Love*. Eva lives in California with her husband, Bill, who actively supports and encourages her new writing career.

Books by Eva Rutland

HARLEQUIN ROMANCE
2897—TO LOVE THEM ALL
2944—AT FIRST SIGHT

HARLEQUIN REGENCY ROMANCE
1—MATCHED PAIR
20—THE VICAR'S DAUGHTER

NO ACCOUNTING FOR LOVE

Eva Rutland

Harlequin Books

TORONTO • NEW YORK • LONDON
AMSTERDAM • PARIS • SYDNEY • HAMBURG
STOCKHOLM • ATHENS • TOKYO • MILAN

ISBN 0-373-03064-9

Harlequin Romance first edition July 1990

CHAPTER ONE

CLAY KENCADE STRODE rapidly back and forth across the plush carpet of his private office in the Kencade Building's luxurious penthouse suite. He stopped his pacing a moment to gaze out the window at New York's Fifth Avenue, sixty-four stories below. Then, impatiently, he resumed walking. Cranston was holding him up! It was bad enough that he'd have to spend hours poring over figures, a procedure the meticulous accountant insisted on before he began each audit.

This morning he had already wasted half an hour just waiting for Philip Cranston. Kencade reached across the desk to push the intercom button, glancing only briefly at his picture in the current issue of *Time*. *Clay Kencade, Thirty-Six-Year-Old Millionaire—A Man and His Luck*. He hadn't read the story, but he wanted to tell them that luck had nothing to do with his success. It was timing. Making the right move at the right time and not wasting that precious commodity, he thought as he barked into the intercom.

"Maggie, call and find out what the hell happened to Cranston."

"I've already phoned, Mr. K.," Maggie answered, her voice smooth and unruffled. "Mr. Cranston is ill and they're sending a Ms Rogers in his place. She'll be here directly."

The knowledge that Cranston's replacement was a woman mellowed Clay Kencade considerably. He liked women. In the world of international commerce, predominantly male, Kencade maintained an easy rapport with all the hard-hitting, no-nonsense men like himself. But even in business, women were... well, like a breath of fresh air. He had found that, almost without exception, the business women he encountered showed an eagerness, an intense dedication, as well as proficiency in their fields. He liked the way they looked, too, so chic and well put together, yet so alluringly feminine, surrounded by a delicate aroma of expensive perfume.

Yes, he liked the feminine touch. But he preferred his meetings with female associates to be dinner conferences, sometimes extended into full evenings if the woman was particularly charming and the conversation especially delightful. So this Ms Rogers was a little late. Probably stopped to fix her makeup or comb her hair or something. Maybe they could continue their discussion through a late lunch.

SHE KNEW SHE WAS LATE but she didn't care. Cynthia Rogers sat at her desk staring at the phone. She would not budge from her office until the pediatrician called.

"Cindy, you're ruining your manicure again," Jane called from across the cubicle the two of them shared at the office of Carruthers and Cranston.

Cindy looked down. Darn! She was biting her thumbnail again.

"Oh, Jane, Jamey had a fever last night—102 degrees. It was gone by this morning, but I am a little worried."

"You've done nothing but worry since your sister's kids landed in your lap. If one of them so much as stubs a toe you go off the deep end."

"Well, a fever isn't a stubbed toe!" She knew she sounded defensive. "I...well, I thought I should keep him home today. I'm going to have the doctor look at him. I wasn't even coming in to the office today, except to pick up the Alston file. And darn it, now I've got to go on the interview for Cranston."

"Poor baby." Jane said it mockingly, but Cindy hardly noticed. "Children are always getting sniffles and fevers. They have them one day and they're fine the next. Anyway, you said the fever was gone this morning. Why don't you schedule the appointment for tomorrow? Suppose he asks you to lunch."

Cindy looked blank. "Who?"

"Who?" Jane mimicked. "How can you sit there chewing on your fingernails instead of going into raptures! And why don't you put on some lipstick? You're about to have an interview with *Clay Kencade*."

"Oh, you..." Cindy laughed. Jane Bowers was a good accountant, but less interested in her columns of figures than in the clients—especially male clients in the higher tax brackets.

"Lucky, lucky you!" Jane heaved a great sigh. "Wish I could get within speaking distance of him."

"For goodness' sake, why?" Cindy concentrated on stuffing the Kencade file she had assembled for Cranston into her briefcase.

"Need you ask? You of all people are familiar with his P and L. And I suppose you've read this." She held up a copy of *Time*.

"Oh, yeah, I've read it. And I know all about his profit and loss figures." *Luck* was right, she thought. And some day that luck might run out. Because Clay Kencade took entirely too many risks. She'd been doing his audit for four years now, and often had the feeling that the Kencade empire was tottering on the brink. But she didn't discuss clients' business, even with fellow workers, so she said nothing of this to Jane. "A lot of good those millions would do you," she teased. "He's not the marrying kind." *Time* had stated that he was a confirmed bachelor.

"Oh, I wasn't thinking of community property." Jane took out her compact and began to freshen her makeup. "I'd settle for a diamond bracelet or a vacation in Hawaii. He's known to be quite generous."

"Indeed. At least according to rumor. Generous to *all* his ladies."

"Oh, I don't mind the crowd," Jane mumbled as she applied lipstick. "I'd even settle for the luncheon or dinner date you're going to get. Clay Kencade has an edge over most of our wealthy clients. He's also young and handsome!"

"Oh, Jane, you're the most—" Cindy broke off her chuckle to grab her ringing phone. Yes, Dr. Scofield could see Jamey at two-thirty. Cindy made a swift calculation. Ten-fifteen now. If she finished with Kencade by eleven or eleven-thirty at the latest, she could make the twelve-twenty to Connecticut. That would give her plenty of time.

As she picked up her briefcase, she realized that her slacks and loafers were hardly proper attire for a business interview. Oh, well, maybe her silk blouse and blazer would get her by. Giving the matter no further thought, she ran out to hail a cab.

Although Cynthia had been in the Kencade Building several times, she'd never gone above the sixty-third floor, which housed the accounting section of Kencade Enterprises. Nor had she met Clay Kencade in person. According to *Business World* he was a financial wizard. According to the tabloids he was a playboy. And judging by his pictures, he was tall, dark and handsome. But to Cynthia

Rogers, he was a set of figures on a profit and loss statement. Figures that balanced precariously, leaning, in her opinion, toward disaster.

"I try to give him a few hints," Cranston had said to her, "but he doesn't take advice too easily."

Well, I'm not here to give advice. Only to clear up a few things before we start the audit, Cindy thought as the elevator slid to a stop and she entered the luxurious penthouse suite. She smiled as she handed her card to the attractive gray-haired woman behind the desk.

"He's expecting you," said the woman with a friendly nod. "Go right in."

Cindy was accustomed to plush executive suites and to meeting important and powerful executives. She walked into his office prepared, her hand ready to unsnap the briefcase, her mind skimming over pertinent data. He came toward her smiling and Cindy's breath caught in her throat. She looked up into a ruggedly handsome face, her gaze held by the intensity in his dark deep-set eyes. The air around her seemed suddenly charged with electricity.

She hadn't known.... Nothing had prepared her for the magnetism, the sheer energy and power that seemed to emanate from him. *It's not luck!* she thought. It's assurance—an overwhelming confidence that defies anything he touches to fail.

But something stirred inside her, a feeling so sensuous, so intoxicating, that it frightened her. She was consumed by an exciting expectancy and couldn't take her eyes from his crooked smile. Just watching it sent a warm glow through her.

His smile faded as he regarded the small figure, the tousled hair, the loafers. She looked as if she had just walked off a college campus. He swore under his breath.

What the hell did Carruthers mean, sending him an inexperienced neophyte?

She knew exactly what he was thinking, and the knowledge helped bring her jumbled emotions under some kind of control. "Good morning, Mr. Kencade. I'm Cynthia Rogers," she said, taking the initiative as she always did with new clients who discounted her as a rank beginner. "I'm afraid I'm a bit late."

"Thirty-five minutes late to be exact!" And she hadn't spent the time refreshing her makeup, he thought. That sprinkle of freckles across her nose was devoid of cover-up. "I don't like to waste time," he snapped.

He was being so arrogant she wanted to stick out her tongue! But... "Sorry. Traffic jam in the elevator," she said with only a trace of impudence in her voice.

He saw the flicker of defiance in her clear hazel eyes and read it distinctly. *I'm not intimidated by you, Clay Kencade!* Hell, he wasn't trying to intimidate anybody! He was just—

The apology came quickly, as if she'd read his thoughts. "I did stop to make a phone call. It was rather urgent. I hope you haven't been too inconvenienced."

"Well, I do run a tight schedule." He was irritated by her casual manner and found himself wishing for Cranston. Although the man always tied him up for hours, involving him in a detailed discussion of the pros and cons of even the smallest financial move, at least Cranston knew his business. But this child... He sighed, then suddenly realized he was being discourteous. "Won't you have a seat, Ms Rogers?"

She sat in the chair he indicated and looked up at him.

"I do appreciate your coming over." He hesitated then, pondering how to put it kindly. "Nothing to do with you personally," he said, staring down at her hair, a strange mixture of brown and gold. The thick curls fell just right, framing her oval face. "But Kencade Enterprises is a rather complicated business."

She nodded.

"We have extensive holdings in various countries throughout the world." Watching her nod again, he continued, "All these countries have their own individual trade and tax regulations. Only a person with a thorough knowledge of international law could put it all together."

"Of course," she agreed.

"Cranston is familiar with my operation. And I'm rather upset that he's unavailable at such a crucial time."

"Viruses," she said deadpan. "They have no consideration."

He frowned at her sarcasm and a smile softened her face.

"I know just how you feel. Mr. Cranston should be back in a week, or two at the most. We can file for an extension, if you'd prefer to wait."

"That might be a good idea," he said with quick relief. He did like to keep things on schedule, and a delay might mean postponing his trip to London. But without Cranston... He studied her tumbled hair with its different colors. Sun bleached. A sign of more time spent outdoors than bent over ledgers. "I think I would prefer to wait for Cranston," he said. "Sorry you made the trip for nothing."

"No problem. That's my job." She stood, hesitated. Then she looked up at him, her expression serious and wide-eyed. "There are some decisions you should make immediately, Mr. Kencade. Are you going to drop the options on the Peruvian oil leases and...oh, yes, the stock options on Scandinavian Shipping Lines. Some deals need to be wrapped up before the end of the quarter because they're going to affect your tax status.''

He glared at her in astonishment. Then he pointed a firm finger at the chair she had just vacated. ''Sit down, Ms Rogers.''

She sat, complacent and unperturbed by his baleful stare.

''Just tell me one thing, young lady. And wipe that innocent look off your face. Why have you been putting me on?''

''I am not responsible for the assumptions you make concerning my qualifications, Mr. Kencade,'' she answered calmly.

''You might have been courteous enough to inform me.''

''If you had confidence in Carruthers and Cranston, it would not be necessary to inform you that I've been a C.P.A. for five years, and that for the past four years, it's been my responsibility to maintain your files and draft your final papers for the audit and tax returns. As a matter of fact, it's always been Mr. Cranston's policy to have an hour's briefing with me before his interviews with you.''

''I see.'' He regarded her quizzically, somewhat warmed by the wholesome grin that made her look like a mischievous boy. And more amused than angry at his own mistake. He glanced at the clock on the wall behind her. ''Well, since you took thirty-five minutes to get here and ten more to present your credentials, that doesn't leave us much time. Would you mind waiting until after my next appointment? Then we could discuss any important data over lunch.''

''I'm sorry, but that's not possible. I have another appointment, too. Anyway,'' she added, ''it shouldn't take us long. I'm pretty well up on things. There are just a few details I need your immediate decisions on.'' She drew some papers from her briefcase. "Look at this," she said, placing a sheet before him.

He sat down behind his desk and looked reluctantly at the papers. He hated this procedure. Hated to focus on tiny figures that spelled profit and loss, such abstract concepts to him. His focus was on the real things—the bankrupt hardware chain or the failing automobile factory and the action that would make a difference. Buy. Sell. Change or expand. He moved a little restlessly in his chair and she went on with the data.

He had to admit she was well prepared. As meticulous as Cranston but somehow more at ease. Cranston had a tendency to vacillate about future options and always engaged in long discussions pertaining to each venture. Cynthia Rogers offered no advice, but her precise analysis of essential facts and cost figures left him free to make his own decisions. He liked that.

"Well, I think that about wraps it up for now," she said some time later.

"Yes, you had everything well organized." He gave her a speculative look. She really was quite attractive in a fresh, unadorned sort of way. "Sure you can't stay for lunch?"

"No, I'm sorry," she said, not even glancing at him as she reached across the desk to gather her scattered papers. He caught a faint delicate scent of... baby powder? He glanced quickly at her hand. The fingers were slender, ink smudged and ringless. One thumbnail was bitten to the quick. There was something insecure and vulnerable about her, no matter how capable she appeared.

"It wouldn't delay you too much," he said. "We can eat here in the executive dining room."

"Thank you, but no. I really do have another appointment." Decisively she snapped her briefcase shut and smiled at him. "Anyway, I think we have everything in order. I shouldn't have to trouble you again until I'm ready for your signature. Well, goodbye, Mr. Kencade. Uh... have a nice day," she stammered, hurrying out of his office.

She managed to walk sedately past the secretary, but once she was in the outer hall she ran toward the elevator. What was she running from? she wondered as she feverishly pushed the down button. But she knew.

Clay Kencade.

She'd been totally unprepared for the impact of his physical presence. Unprepared for her own vibrant response—a warm exhilarating anticipation that still stirred within her as the elevator slid downward. She had not felt that way since Dan.

No, be honest, Cindy. Dan had never evoked this kind of strange emotion. The moment she looked into Clay Kencade's dark eyes, she'd felt strangely shaken, disoriented. Thank goodness she'd been able to hide her reaction! She was accustomed to clients who, seeing her for the first time, invariably associated her youthful appearance with incompetence. She always assumed a brisk, businesslike air and delighted in proving them wrong.

Past experience had been today's salvation. She'd hidden her intense personal feelings behind a mask of professionalism. The notes and balance sheets she had pulled from her briefcase had steadied her hand and cleared her brain. She had not faltered through the business-as-usual routine.

The luncheon invitation had almost thrown her. She had a compelling desire to be with him, to really know him. This strong and unexpected feeling was unnerving and it contradicted her firm resolve not to become involved with any man.

Involved? She often had lunch or even the occasional dinner conference with male associates or clients. Why would a lunch with Kencade be different?

But she knew it would. She felt an unmistakable sense of apprehension and quickly told herself that Cranston would be back soon to take over the Kencade file. It probably wouldn't be necessary to see Kencade again. *That's a relief,* she muttered fiercely.

With practical deliberation she turned her mind to more immediate concerns. She checked her watch. Eleven-forty-five. She'd be able to catch the twelve-twenty and get Jamey to the doctor in time.

Maybe Jane was right, she thought, as she ran out of the building and hailed a cab. Perhaps she *was* unduly concerned about the three children who'd become her responsibility when her sister, Claire, died a little more than a year ago. It seemed longer. Teri, the girl, had been a baby. Now she was almost three and her brothers—Johnny was nine and Jamey five. They were growing fast and Cindy could hardly keep up.

She sighed. She knew she was too intense, but she couldn't seem to help it. She wished she could be more like Claire, who had been a delightful and totally relaxed mother. That is, until the awful months preceding her death.

Seated in the cab, Cindy watched the driver maneuver his way through the traffic and thought about Claire. Had Claire's illness been brought on by stress? Her emotions must have been in turmoil for some time, but there had been no indication of the disease until three months after her husband's fatal automobile crash. His death had been a double shock to Claire, for the accident had occurred not in California, where he was supposed to be on a business trip, but on the Pennsylvania Turnpike, where he was accompanied by his pretty secretary.

The whole incident had been a shock to Cindy, too. She'd always considered her sister's marriage to John Atwood a solid one, although her visits to their home had been infrequent. Cindy had been completely absorbed in her own very full life. Happy in her small Manhattan apartment. Happy with her successful accounting career. Happy and in love with Dan, her fiancé.

"You don't mean you're taking the children!" Dan had exclaimed as he helped her through the aftermath of legal entanglements.

"Of course I am," she had answered in some surprise. "Who else?"

Not her own parents, who had sold their Bronx home five years before and moved to an adult retirement community in Phoenix, Arizona, where the climate would be more beneficial for her mother's arthritis.

Not Jerry, Cindy's younger brother, in his last year at law school in California.

Not John's parents, Claire's in-laws had never evidenced much interest in their son, much less their three grandchildren.

"We do want to help," John's mother had said. "We might take the baby girl," she added doubtfully. "But at this time of our life . . . Oh, I just couldn't cope with a boy again."

As if Cindy would allow the children to be separated! Nor would she have given any of them to that doubtful woman.

"You can see that I've got to take them," she had said to Dan.

"Yes," he'd agreed. And he *had* been helpful, Cindy admitted now as she left the cab and hurried through the crowded station. Dan had helped her move from the apartment to Claire's big house in Greenwich, Connecticut, since of course it wasn't practical to move the children. Dan had spent many weekends with them, too, taking the boys sailing and romping with them in the big yard. And he had done it cheerfully. For six whole months. Then he had given up.

"It's not that you've taken the children," he told Cindy. "It's more like they've taken you."

There had been some truth in that, she admitted as she found a seat on the train. No more evenings spent with Dan at the theater. No more late dinners and dancing until two in the morning. No private togetherness in her little apartment. Maybe if they hadn't postponed their marriage . . . Or if she hadn't been as dedicated to her job as she was to the children . . .

But perhaps it had all been for the best. Although she'd thought she loved Dan, she hardly missed him now. Not nearly as much as the boys did. For them it had been yet another desertion.

Cindy sighed again, wishing she could be as relaxed as Claire, as carefree as Dan. She tried. She really did. She was always so careful with the children. She played tag ball with them, read to them as they ate popcorn before the big stone fireplace, kissed and coddled baby Teri, and the boys, too, as much as they would let her.

But life was not just loving and playing games. Cindy keenly felt the weight of responsibility for the three lives so dependent on her. She tried to organize for the children's care and discipline as efficiently as she organized her ledgers. But there was a difference. She could juggle millions of dollars on balance sheets as offhandedly as she put on her shoes. And she could do it with confidence, knowing her figures were correct.

But she just couldn't seem to handle the children with that same ease or confidence. She hadn't let Johnny play soccer because she felt it was too dangerous. Now she'd let him sign up for baseball and he was so excited. Was it right to keep him from practice until he brought up his math grades? And what about today, Jamey? She was bothered by a slight feeling of guilt. She'd kept him home from school and was leaving work early to check on him when maybe he wasn't really ill.

Relax, she told herself firmly. Then, remembering that she didn't like to waste the forty-five-minute train ride, she opened her briefcase and took out some papers. As she looked at the notes in the margin written in that heavy decisive scrawl, her breath caught and again she felt the strange excitement stirring in her breast.

CHAPTER TWO

"THIS LOOKS like a healthy young lad to me," said Dr. Scofield. "Are you sure you weren't just trying to skip school, Jamey?"

"Cindy wouldn't let me go. And I wanted to, on account of today we were going to the park." Jamey looked at Cindy reproachfully as he squirmed off the examining table. Then he pushed back the thatch of blond hair that was always falling in his face and announced, "I didn't cry."

"No. But you didn't get a shot, either," the doctor said, his eyes twinkling.

"Well, do I get a balloon anyway?"

"Jamey!" Cindy protested, straightening his shirt and trying to comb his hair into some kind of order. He needed a haircut.

Dr. Scofield laughed as he told Jamey to see the nurse and collect his balloon. Then he turned to Cindy. "So it's just a case of an overanxious aunt again, huh?" Cindy smiled sheepishly and thanked him, gathering up her purse and Jamey's coat.

I'm tired of people telling me I'm too anxious, she thought, as she shepherded Jamey into Claire's old station wagon. *I just want to do what's right for them.* To do what Claire would have done. To make sure they were—

"Can we stop and get a hamburger and a shake, Cindy?"

"No, we can't. And buckle your seat belt."

"Aw..."

"Aw..." Cindy mimicked as she leaned over and fastened the belt herself. "We're going out for pizza tonight, remember? Right now we have to get home to do our chores so Mrs. Stewart can leave." Mrs. Stewart, the live-in housekeeper, always spent the weekends with her sister in the city.

"But Cindy, what about your own time off?" Jane had once asked. "Friday, Saturday and Sunday—that's prime dating time."

"Oh, I don't lack for dates!" Cindy gave a little chuckle. "There are swimming lessons and birthday parties and—"

"Oh, you," her coworker had declared. "I don't see how you can stand to be so confined."

"I don't feel confined," Cindy told her. And she didn't. She loved the children, and she enjoyed them. Well, most of the time, anyway. She grinned, thinking that her weekends with them proved more than ever that Mrs. Stewart needed a breather after spending Monday to Friday with the three lively youngsters. Mrs. Stewart was a jewel and she didn't want to lose her, Cindy mused, as she drove up the driveway and into the three-car garage. From the garage she went through the back hall into the big family room, Jamey running in front of her shouting that they were home.

Cindy never failed to be moved by the torrent of love that was showered upon her every time she entered the house. Maybe bombarded was a better word, she thought now as Johnny ran toward her, waving a paper.

"Hi, Cindy! Look. I got a B in my math test. See? I just missed two. Can I go to baseball practice tomorrow? Can I? Look."

"Johnny, that's great! I'm so proud of you." She threw aside her briefcase, but before she could take the paper, little Teri stumbled between them, adding her "Cindy, Cindy" to the chorus. "Hello, pumpkin!" Cindy scooped up the three-year-old and nuzzled her neck while managing to capture and evade the sticky hands that still held a Popsicle.

"Oh, my goodness." Mrs. Stewart stepped from the kitchen and lifted Teri from Cindy's arms. "You're going to get your auntie all messed up. Let's go wash your hands and face."

"You can take an early train," Cindy told the housekeeper. "I'll run up and change, and then I'll drive you to the station."

The children went with her to the station. When they returned, she looked over Johnny's test and had him correct the two questions he'd missed before she marched them all upstairs to do their chores. "We need to get the cleaning done so we can go out for pizza tonight," she reminded them. "You know we leave early tomorrow for baseball."

Mrs. Stewart, who had her own bedroom and bath next to the laundry room, kept the whole downstairs spic-and-span. But it was too much to expect one person to maintain order in the big house with its four bedrooms and baths. No, five, counting the housekeeper's. Too much house. At least that had been Cindy's opinion when she first moved into it from her small apartment, barely larger than the master bedroom suite she now occupied. But, except for the seldom used formal living and dining rooms, their daily activities extended into every inch of the split-level house. Thank goodness for her brother-in-law's mortgage insurance, which had left the house free and clear, enabling Cindy to preserve the children's established routines.

Even so, it wasn't easy. There were still taxes, insurance and maintenance costs, plus the housekeeper's salary and the children's tuition, to say nothing of the food and clothing required for a rapidly growing family. Both sets of grandparents had offered financial aid, but Cindy had said that with John's life insurance and social security they could manage. However, much of John's insurance money had been absorbed by Claire's illness, and Cindy had invested the remainder for the children's college years. She was finding that her salary and John's social security checks could not keep pace with expenses and she was digging into her savings. Still, she didn't want to ask for help. She ought to be able to manage on her own. But she was worried. She'd decided it was best for the boys to remain with the same teachers and classmates, but she might have to remove them from their private school next year, she thought, as she scrubbed bathrooms with Teri's "help," monitored Johnny's vacuuming and insisted that Jamey pick up every scattered toy.

CINDY LOVED springtime in Greenwich. She loved watching the trees burst into new green life, loved the sunny, hopeful days and the air, fresh and tangy with the sweet scent of blossoming things. She breathed in the rich smell of new-mown grass on the Little League baseball diamond when they arrived for Johnny's first practice with the team on which he'd been placed, the Semco Cubs.

She seemed to be the only parent present except for the coach and his wife. The coach, a tall, handsome man everyone called Steve, was having a tough time trying to line up fifteen boys for fielding practice, while yelling at his son and some other strays, "Davey, you guys get off those bleachers and get over here! Pronto!"

"He really needs Lem," said his wife, shaking her head.

"Who's Lem?" Cindy asked.

"He was going to be assistant coach, only he broke his leg and he's out of commission for the whole season. Oh, by the way, I'm Marcy Prescott."

"Cindy Rogers. Can I help?"

Marcy, who was taking each boy's measurements, was finding her task rather difficult, for she was noticeably pregnant.

"Oh, would you?" she asked gratefully. And Cindy took the tape measure while Marcy wrote down names and sizes. "Steve's company is springing for new uniforms," Marcy said. "They're going to be white with *Semco* on the front and the numbers on the back in red. Socks, caps and helmets will also be red."

"Sounds great," said Cindy, glancing around for Teri. The coach's little girl had taken charge of her, and Jamey was tagging along after them.

After they'd finished measuring all the boys, Cindy, who had often played baseball with her brother, Jerry, and his friends, helped the coach with fielding practice. Later, she wondered how she happened to become assistant coach. Maybe it was because Marcy was so pregnant and Steve so harassed. Or maybe it was because Steve said he just needed someone to keep track of the boys and the equipment. Anyway, what did it matter, since she would always be here with Johnny? As Marcy said, "He manages to run a whole company and make decisions without any help, but organizing a group of small boys is another matter altogether."

PHILIP CRANSTON'S SICK LEAVE lasted longer than expected, and on a Monday morning two weeks later, Cindy moved with her audit team into the Kencade Building, where they started work in the section temporarily reserved for them. Kencade Enterprises occupied the top five floors of the Kencade Building; the accounting department was located on the sixty-third. There, late Tuesday afternoon, Cindy stood behind Ted Barrister's chair, peering at the figures he was calling up on his computer screen. Holdings had increased more than ten percent since last quarter, and her orderly accountant's mind boggled at the variety of takeovers, ranging from ships to bathtubs.

Time had called Clay Kencade a brilliant entrepreneur, but *Business World* had labeled him a "scavenger, who fed on the failures of others." Scavenger was an ugly word, but to Cindy there was something greedy about this indiscriminate grabbing of tottering businesses. She shrugged and bent over to make a notation on Ted's work sheet when she sensed it—a stillness, barely perceptible, before the muted clicking of computers and the low murmur of voices began again. She looked up and saw the reason. Clay Kencade.

This was probably the first time the corporation president had appeared in the accounting section. She'd certainly never seen him during any of the several weeks she had spent there with Cranston's team in the past four years. So why was he there now?

The office manager approached him, but Kencade waved her aside and moved directly toward Cindy. She felt breathless and light-headed as once again that strange, tingling expectancy surged through her. She swallowed, braced herself and faced him with what she hoped was a look of calm inquiry. "Good afternoon, Mr. Kencade."

"Ms Rogers. How are things going?" His smile was warm and genial. How could a man who embodied so much power look so relaxed? She resented his calmness in view of her own agitation, which she was trying hard to stifle. What on earth was the matter with her? She saw him nod to Ted, who muttered an excuse and hurried away, leaving the two of them alone—or as alone as they could be in that crowded room.

"You haven't run into any problems, I hope?"

"Oh, no," she said quickly, realizing she hadn't answered his first question. "Everything's going very well so far."

"Good. Well, it's almost closing time. I was wondering, could you join me for an early dinner?"

"I...er..." This was the last thing Cindy had expected. She felt momentarily confused, and surprisingly sorry that she had to decline. "I'm sorry. I have an...appointment."

"Oh. Well, what about lunch tomorrow?"

"I'm sorry. I have—" She stopped. He was one of their most important clients. "Did you have something you wished to discuss, Mr. Kencade?"

He shook his head. "A request, Ms Rogers. Not a command."

"Oh, I didn't think...that is, I wasn't..." Darn! She was acting like a blushing schoolgirl. She could see the laughter in his eyes and spoke almost defiantly. "It's just that tomorrow's our regular staff lunch meeting. Mr. Cranston is still out and I promised to review some matters for him."

"I see." His mouth gave a wry twist. "Well, I'd hate to upset your busy schedule. Perhaps another time." He turned abruptly and strode away.

She felt a stab of disappointment as she watched him depart. Maybe she could have managed tonight.... Oh, for goodness' sake, she was the assistant coach now. She had to be there. Anyway, she'd resolved a long time ago that nothing—absolutely nothing—would interfere with the children's activities. And how was Johnny going to get to practice if she didn't take him?

Still she wished... Not to be without the children, because she loved them dearly. But, well... just for a bit of the old freedom. When there was no urgency to hurry home. When one could linger lazily over a cocktail or dinner, could explore a strange new feeling... get to really know someone.

"Hey, Cindy, look at this!"

She hadn't realized Ted was back, and his voice startled her. She turned again to the screen, but her mind was focused on the man who had just left. A bit of pride stirred within her. He'd asked her out again! He found her attractive, wanted to know her better! But— Her spirits dampened. Jane had predicted that he'd ask her out. Jane, who read all the tabloids, had declared that his personal relationships were reported to be as varied as his business interests. And that they'd never yet been more than short-term.

Short-term. Like Dan's relationship with the children. She would not let them be hurt again.

CLAY KENCADE SHRUGGED as he boarded the private elevator to his penthouse suite. Well, that was that! Or was it? he wondered, as he got out of the elevator and went into his office through the back entrance. The thing was, he hadn't been able to get her out of his mind since she'd first breezed through his door that Friday morning. He really didn't know why.

And he didn't know why, when he'd finally tracked her down in Accounting, she made him feel so... well, face it...awkward. He'd never been awkward with women. Not since he was fourteen.

He smiled to himself, his thoughts going back to the summer he met the three stepsisters who'd made almost bearable the mandatory summer months spent with his mother and her third husband. Jake, his stepfather, was a surly man with a vicious temper. He resented Clay's presence only slightly more than he did that of his own daughters. The visits had been timed simultaneously in order to "get it all over with at once."

However, the girls, one a year older and two slightly younger than Clay, were delighted with the arrangement that brought a male peer into their totally feminine household. They frankly adored this new brother with his blunt male opinions about which outfit did or did not look right on them, who gave advice about other boys, substituted as an escort and made their hair dryer work. To Clay, their companionship and open adoration was a flattering contrast to the Spartan existence he shared with his father during the nine months of the school year. The visits provided a totally innocent but highly engaging introduction to the world of women. This close association had spanned only two summers, but it had had a lasting effect on him. Now, more than twenty years and two stepfathers later, he remained in contact with the three women. Never could he forget their warm sisterly affection and how they had guided him through his first dance steps and the shyness and intricacies of first dating. And never, since that time, had he ever felt uncomfortable with any member of the opposite sex. Except... What did Cynthia Rogers have against him?

He had seen it. That half-defiant, closed-in look.

Anyway, why did he care?

Because there was something different about her. Something behind that strictly businesslike air of hers that—

"Oh, Mr. K.," Maggie said as she came in bearing a sheaf of papers, "why didn't you let me know you were back?"

"Just got here," he answered, tossing his coat and tie onto a sofa and just missing the plant beside it.

"Well, I hope you're staying put for a moment." Maggie was a tall woman whose trim figure, perfect coiffure and Dior suit belied the fact that she was a picture-carrying, cookie-baking, fifty-year-old grandmother. "We need to get some things cleared up," she announced, placing her folders on his desk and seating herself beside it with pad and pencil poised.

"At your service, ma'am." Resignedly Clay sank into his big leather chair and looked attentively at his secretary. But his mind focused on a woman with two-tone tousled hair and a preponderance of appointments.

"The Landover chain rejected your offer," Maggie told him.

"I wonder why," he mused. Did she really have an appointment or was that just an excuse to avoid him?

"Do you want to go higher?"

"Oh, hell, what's the point!" If she didn't like him, if she found him unattractive, why bother?

"Very well." Maggie laid the Landover folder aside. "They might reconsider your bid if they don't get another offer."

"Another offer? Do you think she's involved with someone?" Now, why did that thought bother him?

"Who?" Maggie was consulting her notes.

"Cynthia Rogers."

"Cynthia—" Maggie's puzzled eyes regarded him. "What are you talking about?"

"That accountant Carruthers sent over. Cynthia Rogers."

"Oh?"

"She's a very busy person."

"Oh?"

"Always has some appointment."

"Do you mean to say that this lady has actually had the effrontery—or perhaps I should say guts—to reject one of your spur-of-the-moment invitations?"

"Spur-of—? Oh, Maggie!"

"Spur-of-the-moment, Mr. K. I don't deny that the line of would-be recipients is long. Ladies panting for some notice from you—"

"Oh, will you cut it out!" he muttered, scowling at her.

"But there may be a few," she murmured, unperturbed, "who desire a little advance notice, shall we say...to prepare for the big event. Or perhaps to rearrange their calendars."

"All right. All right. I get the point." He shifted in his chair, acknowledging to himself that most of his moves or requests *were* impulsive. Seldom did he make plans.

"Let's see." Maggie fumbled among the folders. "Oh, yes. Here are the reports from that plant in Denver."

"Reports. You can put anything on paper. I have to *see* the plant. Make an appointment. No, wait. I prefer a surprise visit. How's my schedule for next week?"

Twenty minutes later they had finished and Clay got to his feet. But before he could reach for his jacket, Maggie brought up something else. "There was a call from *Fortune* magazine. They want an interview."

Clay stopped in the middle of a stretch to stare at her. "You know I don't give interviews."

"Well, I think it's high time you did. Otherwise people say what they damn well please, regardless of the facts. According to *Business World*, you're a greedy vulture, taking advantage of people whose lifework crumbles beneath them."

"Sticks and stones," he chanted, waving his finger at her.

"Go ahead and laugh," she said, her face quite red as she stood up. "But there's never a word about how you saved their skins, taking them in as partners or making them managers or giving other incentives. Besides rescuing that crumbling business they didn't know what to do with."

"Maggie, remember your blood pressure."

"Well, I might just give *Fortune* an interview. If you won't defend yourself—"

"Take it easy." He leaned over to kiss her cheek. "No interviews," he said emphatically. "We'll just take care of business and let other people talk."

"Speaking of people—it's a pity you don't read your own press. That gossip magazine, *Personalities,* claims you pursue women the way you do businesses, and that you discard them more quickly. I'd like to get hold of that editor," she grumbled, as she gathered up the folders. "I'd tell her a thing or two."

"Maggie!" He chuckled as he put on his coat. "What brought on this tirade?"

"Well, they ought to know who's pursuing whom! Lord, the women who are trying to...to get their hooks into you—" She broke off as the buzzer on his desk sounded.

In answer to her questioning frown, he lifted an eyebrow and flipped the switch. "Yes?"

"Darling," came a sultry feminine voice, "Maggie's not in here. So I just pushed this little button to see if I could find you. Clay, are you alone?"

"Well, I—er... Yes, just Maggie."

"Oh, I— Oh, for goodness' sake, let me in. I don't want to talk into this machine."

Maggie opened the door and the owner of the voice swept in. A vision in green silk and gabardine, enveloped in an intoxicating aroma of Obsession. She gave Maggie a casual nod, then hurried to Clay.

"Now, Clay, don't tell me you're too busy. I have the most exciting plan. Dinner—I thought perhaps that place you took me last month. And then, if you're very, very good..."

Maggie gave him a what-did-I-tell-you glance before she left the office and quietly shut the door.

AT FOUR-THIRTY Cindy squeezed into a cab with three of her coworkers who were also making connections at Grand Central. She'd told Mrs. Stewart to give the kids an early dinner. All she had to do was change and pick up Johnny, so they should get to the field by six. If she caught the four-forty-seven train, that is. She glanced at the driver, who hadn't yet managed to maneuver his way into the line of traffic.

She had to stop feeling so hurried and anxious! Forcing herself to relax, she leaned back and looked at the throng of people pouring out of the Kencade Building—and saw Clay Kencade with an exceptionally beautiful woman hanging on his arm.

Ignoring the small lump in her throat, Cindy watched them move down the sidewalk. The woman walked slowly, her hips swaying. *But she's sure talking a blue streak,* Cindy thought, as she gazed at the elegant profile, noting the rapid movement of the woman's lips and the radiance of the smile that was lifted to Clay. He matched his steps to hers and bent toward her as if completely engrossed in her every word.

How about an early dinner? he'd asked, not quite an hour ago. It hadn't taken him long to find a replacement. Cindy's face burned as a hot current of resentment raced through her. She was glad she'd turned him down. Glad, too, when the taxi sped past, removing them from her vision.

And she felt irritated that the image remained. A man and a woman, absorbed in each other's company.

It meant nothing to her. Nothing!

CHAPTER THREE

At noon, a few days later, Clay Kencade stepped out of a cab and turned to see Cynthia Rogers leave the building. She strode purposefully down the street and he stood for a moment watching, liking the way she walked—head held high, shoulders straight, swinging along on those slender legs. It seemed to him that she was engaged in some private business, completely unaware of the many admiring glances that followed her steps. She moved quickly and lightly with a natural unstudied grace. Yet her movements were buoyant, as if she felt it a joy to be alive.

When she'd disappeared among the crowd, he hurried into the building, feeling rather embarrassed. He found himself always watching her, watching *for* her. Trying to catch a glimpse as she went striding down the avenue or through the lobby on her way to work or departing for lunch. He hadn't asked her out again and wasn't sure why. It had nothing to do with Maggie's crack that she was the only woman who'd ever turned him down. That was quite untrue.

Or was it? he wondered as he got into the elevator. Hell, he couldn't remember! It had never seemed to matter before.

Why did it matter now?

Once he'd seen her in the downstairs coffee shop with some guy from Accounting. She had looked up at the man, her eyes sparkling, as they laughed and talked so easily together. Clay had felt a fierce unreasoning surge of envy. Crazy. He hardly knew her. And she hardly knew him. So why did she . . . well, back off? Her refusal of both his invitations had been so definite, so unequivocal . . . and so smoothly polite. *I'm sorry. I have an appointment.*

Well, he thought, grinning as he got off the elevator, *I'll fix that!*

"What was that crack you made, Maggie, something about spur of the moment?" he asked when he went into the office.

Maggie looked up, puzzled. "Now what are you talking about?"

"Never mind. Take a letter."

Later Maggie smiled as she typed the semiformal invitation. Mr. Clay Kencade requests the pleasure of Ms Cynthia Rogers's company at a time and on such date as Ms Rogers finds suitable and convenient. RSVP by checking appropriate box:

Dinner, Saturday, April 14 at 7:00 p.m.

Brunch, Sunday, April 15 at 10:00 a.m.

Lunch, Monday, April 16 at noon . . .

There were several other alternative dates, and Maggie chuckled to herself. Mr. K. was always persistent about anything he really wanted. Ms Rogers would have to dream up an abundance of appointments to politely refuse this invitation.

As she walked into Woolworths, Cindy's step was purposeful, but her thoughts skittered from one subject to another—Teri's birthday, Johnny's teeth, her budget. And a man named Sam Alexander.

She selected Teri's presents, choosing a tiny purse containing a play makeup kit (*she'll like that*), a jigsaw puzzle, crayons and coloring books (*two, so she can share with*

Jamey). Teri had a problem about sharing, she thought. And she was spoiled because the boys gave in to her. *I'll have to find a play group soon or get her into nursery school,* Cindy decided, as she handed her purchases to the clerk. There was a nursery at the boys' school, but...darn! All that tuition.

And Johnny was due for braces this fall; the dentist had said he should be fitted when he was ten. Three thousand dollars. And the insurance would pay only half.

"Thank you," she said, smiling as she took her package from the salesclerk. She put her change in her purse and started back to the office, then remembered the man who'd stepped into the elevator as she got out.

Sam Alexander. She'd seen him there before. One day the week before he'd boarded the elevator with her and pushed the button for the Kencade executive suite. He had spoken and she'd nodded, for she knew him. He was the principal owner and financial manager of a paper company on the West side that had filed for bankruptcy about a month earlier. He was one of Carruthers and Cranston's clients, and Philip Cranston had sent Cynthia to do the paperwork. She hadn't liked what she'd seen.

"It looks as if the figures have been fiddled with," she'd told Cranston. "It appears that someone's been siphoning off the profits." Probably burying them in some Swiss bank account.

"Careful, honey," Cranston had said. "We're not investigators. And we don't blow the whistle on clients. Just deal with the figures they give you. Carefully," he'd added, winking at her.

So that was what she had done. But she didn't like it. And she didn't trust Sam Alexander. He had small shifty eyes that signaled a warning as distinctive as the rattle of a poisonous snake.

Still, she might never have thought of him again had she not run into him. Twice. And right here, she thought as she went back into the Kencade Building and took the elevator to Accounting. *I'll bet my bottom dollar he's trying to palm off his decrepit paper mill on Kencade Enterprises.*

And he might very well succeed, the way Clay Kencade ran his business. Really, that man was an enigma to her. Not only did he pick up firms on the very edge of disaster, more often than not he signed on with the same people who'd created the disaster in the first place, sometimes even forming partnerships with them. So far he'd been incredibly lucky. But if he took on a man like Sam Alexander... She really ought to warn him.

Oh, sure. Just walk up out of the clear blue and say "I saw this man in the elevator...and I *thought* you might be making a deal with him.... I *think* he's ... well, shady."

She'd look like a perfect idiot.

Oh, for goodness' sake, she thought, what was one rotten apple in the barrel of firms owned by Clay Kencade! Anyway, he was a big boy. He could look after himself.

Yet, for all that, for all his confidence and power, there was something about him. Something, well, trusting. Maybe too trusting.

It was then that she reached her desk and saw the envelope addressed to her. She opened it.

"Mr. Clay Kencade requests the pleasure of..."

It was so very different. Clever. And funny. Giving her—she counted—ten choices! A man like Clay Kencade. He was the one with all the appointments, business and other things, she thought, remembering the woman with the swaying hips.

She looked at the list again. It was as if he really wanted to see her, and that made her feel...special.

Careful, Cindy! She didn't have time to get involved and— Oh, what difference did one evening make! In fact, as she again consulted her choices, Thursday night seemed to be her only available time. She started to check it, then stopped. This was such an unusual approach.

She refolded the paper, put it back into the envelope and tucked it carefully in her purse. Then she typed her reply. "Ms Cynthia Rogers accepts Mr. Kencade's kind invitation with pleasure...."

When he phoned to ask where he should pick her up, she suggested they meet in the lobby at six-thirty. She would do a little overtime work rather than rush home first, she decided. She felt a little guilty about the children—she couldn't help it. But she'd ask Mrs. Stewart to give them a treat after supper. And it wasn't as though she did this often, Cindy told herself firmly.

THE PLEASURE CLAY FELT when he saw Cindy waiting in the lobby surprised him. He'd been half-afraid she'd change her mind.

She was concentrating on a brochure in her hand and had not yet seen him. Her dress, a lightweight knit of rich brown, was sleeveless with simple straight lines; it enhanced her small but well-proportioned figure. She wore brown leather pumps, and a slit in the dress provocatively revealed her slender legs with the trim little ankles.

He'd reserved a table at the Ritz, but when she looked up at him and smiled he changed his mind. Suddenly he didn't want to share her.

Cindy was surprised when the taxi rounded Central Park and turned west on Eighty-seventh into what was definitely a residential area. It stopped in front of one of the old brownstones.

Faded glory, she thought, surveying the neighborhood while he paid the cabdriver. Old apartments or large houses that had been converted into apartments. Not posh, but neat and well cared for. A few people milled about, coming and going. Cars were being parked alongside the curb. Coming-home time.

Why are we here, anyway?

As the taxi sped away she felt a stab of apprehension. She turned quickly to Kencade. "It was my understanding that we were going to dinner."

"We are."

"Here?" She could see nothing resembling a restaurant.

"The food's great." His smile was teasing. "Quiet atmosphere. Excellent chef..." He took her arm to lead her up to the small portico.

She didn't move. "Just who is this excellent chef?"

He clicked his heels, inclined his head, still grinning.

"You? But you can't...you don't..." She glanced at the modest brownstone. Certainly not the setting she would have expected for Clay Kencade. "You—this is where you live?"

He nodded.

"I don't think I..." She hesitated, not wanting to appear prudish, but not liking the look of this. He was regarding her solemnly now, the teasing smile gone. "I think I'd prefer to—to go to a restaurant," she finished rather lamely.

"Why don't you say what you really mean?"

"I—I did."

"Well, your eyes said something different, like 'Look, buster, I'm not about to be stuck in some apartment alone with you. Not when all I know about you is what I read in the tabloids—which is not exactly the best recommendation!'"

"Please," she whispered, glancing at a passerby who had hesitated. It must look as if they were quarreling.

"I'm sorry." He lowered and softened his voice. "Look, if we go upstairs, you set the rules. If you don't want me to come within arm's length of you, I won't. I'll stay clear across the room if you want. And, to be honest, I did make reservations at the Ritz. We can still go there if you'd rather. But when I came down into the lobby and you looked at me and smiled—suddenly I wanted you all to myself this evening. Now, will you let me cook for you?" He held out his hand. "I promise to be a gentleman."

His gaze was so frank and open, his words so sincere, that she couldn't help the tug of response, full of warmth and trust. She put her hand in his and together they walked toward the portico.

The door was held for them by an attendant, an older man not in uniform but wearing a dark suit. He nodded affably. "Good evening, Mr. Kencade." Clay cordially returned his greeting and the man retreated to his desk in one corner of the sizable entry hall with its polished marble floors.

They took the old-fashioned elevator to the top floor. Cindy felt both nervous and strangely excited as she stood beside Clay in the small enclosure. In less than a minute, they'd arrived. Clay opened the door and led her into the apartment.

She found herself standing in a spacious, well-appointed living room decorated in strong, earthy colors. Neat and clean, but with a lived-in look—a coffee cup and open newspaper on the table by the window, a pair of jogging shoes askew on the floor in front of the sofa.

"So this is your place," she said, imagining him jogging around the park in the morning and returning to his newspaper and coffee. Just an ordinary man. Unlike the god in the penthouse office.

"All mine. Make yourself comfortable." He picked up the shoes and disappeared into what she assumed was the bedroom.

Cindy, realizing that she was about to bite her thumbnail, put her hands resolutely behind her and wandered restlessly about, determined to be as calm and self-assured as he. She walked over to the fireplace, looked at the large fern in a brass pot on the hearth, studied the painting over the mantel. A stylized skyline of the city, with a great orange sunset casting its glow over Brooklyn Bridge. A good painting. Tasteful, like the rest of the furnishings. He must have had a good decorator. Still, she'd have thought his home would be more luxurious, more ostentatious, befitting his fame and fortune.

"How about a before-dinner drink?" he asked as he reappeared. He had discarded his coat and tie and was rolling up his shirtsleeves. "What's your preference?"

"Whatever the house is pushing," she answered, expecting a martini.

In this, too, she was surprised. He went into the kitchen and she heard the blender whirring. He came back carrying two frothy oversize daiquiris, frosty with crushed ice.

"Delicious," she said, liking the fresh peach taste. She had settled back in a big leather armchair and she looked across at Clay, seated on the sofa with his long legs stretched in front of him. His eyes were intent upon her, and once again she felt that little stir of excitement. But she didn't feel threatened this time. She felt a quiet and sweet exhilaration, as cozy and intimate as the apartment itself.

"This is nice." She made a little gesture with her hand. "Comfortable. And yet not at all what I—" She stopped.

"Not what you expected?" he prompted, his smile a little mocking.

"Well, I..." she faltered. "Well, at least a manservant, puttering around, mixing the drinks."

"That would bug the hell out of me. Couldn't stand someone underfoot all the time."

"Oh. Is that why you've never married?" Darn! She should bite her tongue. The last thing she wanted to do was pry.

"Oh, I wouldn't mind that kind of someone," he said, grinning. "But marriage...well, that usually means children."

She sat up, instantly alert. "You don't like children?"

He shrugged. "I just think marriage is hard on children."

"That's a stupid thing to say!" Still, she thought, Claire's marriage had been hard on *her* children. Yet if Claire and John hadn't married, there wouldn't have *been* any children. "I think marriage is the usual prelude to—"

"Okay, okay." He held up a hand. "Maybe I'm thinking of the usual aftermath. Divorce."

"Oh?"

"And I'm speaking from the vast experience of a child who had to deal with four stepfathers."

"Four!" She almost choked on her drink.

"Well, not all at the same time."

She tried to digest the idea. Falling in love with and marrying four, no, five men! "Your mother must have been very...very attractive," she said, rather awkwardly.

"She still is," he said, and laughed. "She's living in Paris with her fifth. And probably her best. Not counting Pop, of course."

"Oh." She could think of nothing else to say.

He stood up. "I'd better see what the chef has for dinner."

She kicked off her shoes and followed him into the kitchen, which she was surprised to find quite modern, complete with dishwasher, microwave oven and lots of gleaming counters.

"Nice," she said again, watching him remove the thawed steaks from the microwave. "How long have you lived here?"

"About twenty-five years," he answered as he scrubbed two potatoes.

"You're kidding!"

"Nope. Pop and I moved here after the divorce." He oiled the potatoes and punctured the skins with a fork. "After he died . . . well, I just stayed on."

"You lived with your father?"

"He wanted me to learn the business. And that was a break, since I only had to deal with stepfathers during the summer months I spent with my mother."

"Oh." She looked around. "It seems so modern. You must have renovated."

"I bought the building about five years ago. I wanted to update the heating and a few things. Put in central air-conditioning."

Of course. That would be easy enough for him to do. But he hadn't moved. Maybe that meant he wanted to keep his feet on the ground. Or stay close to his roots or something. He had placed the potatoes in the microwave, set the timer and turned on the oven. Now he was chopping fresh asparagus into small pieces.

"You make cooking look easy," she said. She and the children survived on pizza and hamburgers when Mrs. Stewart was away.

He said he'd started cooking when he was about twelve, mainly because his dad couldn't. She said she had never cooked because first there was her mother, then her older sister, Claire. She told him about Claire and her brother, Jerry.

She did not tell him about Claire's children.

While they talked, he made a salad and mixed a vinaigrette dressing, broiled the steaks and sautéed the asparagus. Her contribution was to clear off the polished dining-room table and arrange the silver and wineglasses. As she did so, she thought of Jane. What would she think of this date? No posh restaurant, no posh apartment. Nor had Clay made a pass. *At least not yet,* she thought, feeling herself blush.

She found a candle and placed it on the table. "For atmosphere," she told him.

He nodded, moving toward the stereo. "Music?"

"No," she said quickly. "I like the quiet." What she liked was talking with him.

"So tell me about you," he said, when they were seated.

"I did."

"No, you didn't. You told me about your parents. About your sister who died. About your brother in law school."

"Oh, well, there's not much to tell. New York City College. Carruthers and Cranston. That's about it."

"No personal involvements?" he asked, refilling her wineglass.

"Nothing serious." She paused. "Well, just one. But it's all over."

"Regrets?"

She shook her head. The fact that he seemed really interested made her want to share, to tell him about Dan and how the boys missed him. Johnny's problems with math and the way he loved baseball. And Jamey's fear of water.

Careful, Cindy! You're on your own. Don't involve another man who'll end up hurting the children again. She searched frantically for a change of subject. Business. "Kencade Enterprises has really expanded. Even in the past three months," she offered brightly.

"Bigger is better, so they say."

"Maybe. But you see..." She bit her lip. This was a social evening. Not the time, nor was it her place, to tell him he could run into trouble sinking so much capital into projects that were going nowhere. Maybe Cranston could give him a hint.

Kencade was looking at her over his wineglass, waiting for her to finish what she'd started to say. "Well, um, some of the acquired projects—Scandinavian Shipping Lines is one—are doing well. Profits up forty percent." It was only a small fleet but he'd refurbished the ships and started a tour line. "That was a good buy," she finished.

"But some—Allen's Paints, for instance—are not?"

"Well..." She hesitated, smiling. "Past records and balance sheets tell their own story. Are you allergic to figures or something? Because you don't seem to pay any attention to—"

"All right. I see what you mean." He chuckled. "Let's just say I like people more. Les Allen once worked for my father."

"Oh." A friend. Or at least someone he knew. That explained it. But other people, like Sam Alexander... Should she warn him? Could she?

"You were right." She lifted her wineglass. "To an excellent chef. I didn't even know it was possible to sauté asparagus. It's delicious."

"Thank you. I hoped you'd enjoy...everything. Are you glad you came?"

"Oh, yes," she said quickly. He seemed different. Here, in this modest setting, his shirt rumpled, a lock of his hair falling across his face like Jamey's, he looked unguarded. Trusting.

She took a deep breath. Suddenly, perhaps inexplicably, she felt a need to protect him.

"There was a man in the elevator the other day. A Mr. Alexander."

"Yes," he said, cutting into his steak. "He has a defunct paper company."

She knew it. "And he wants you to invest."

"Something like that."

"Don't." Her tone was so sharp that he jerked his head up.

"You know something against him?"

"Not really." She bit her lip and toyed with her asparagus. *We don't blow the whistle on clients.* "I . . . there's something about him. I don't like his eyes."

"His eyes?" Kencade's brows went up and he chuckled. "Well, maybe I'd better take a good look when I see him again! Coffee?"

"Yes, please." She knew he was discounting what she said. Still, it wasn't her business. Not really.

After dinner, they sat and talked. About everything— books, world affairs, movies, politics, ideas. Cindy felt more relaxed than she had in a long time. She was shocked to glance at her watch, and notice the time. In midsentence she said, "I think you'd better call me a cab. I have to make the last train."

"Train?"

"I live in Greenwich. Connecticut," she added, seeing the question in his eyes.

"Oh, I didn't know. I'd better send for the car."

Of course he would have a car, even though he always seemed to be riding in cabs. "You needn't bother. I leave my own car at the Greenwich station. I'll be quite all right."

He leaned forward and touched his finger to her chin, and a little tremor shot through her. "When I take a lady to dinner, I always see her home."

The Jaguar shone sleek and silver gray in the moonlight. He was as relaxed and confident in his driving as in everything else, and she settled back against the cushions as he eased the car into the flow of traffic. They rode in companionable silence, as if each was savoring the evening. She marveled that she felt such comfort with him. Once he reached over and took her hand, and the comfort grew into something sweet and intimate. She wanted the ride to last a long, long time.

But that was unrealistic. Her emotions were under control by the time they arrived at the station where she would pick up her car. However, he still insisted that he would "see her home," and when she turned into her driveway the Jaguar followed.

She stopped just short of the garage and got out of the car to see him walking toward her. She held out her hand. "It was a delightful evening," she said, and meant it. "Thank you."

"It *was* delightful," he repeated. He bent to kiss her. The touch of his lips on hers was light and surprisingly gentle. Yet it sent a tremor of desire pulsing through her, so strong that she wanted to throw her arms around him and cling. She forced herself to pull away.

"Thank you again," she managed to say quite calmly before she got back into her car and drove into the garage, shutting the door behind her.

CHAPTER FOUR

CLAY STOOD for a moment after the garage door slammed, looking at the house and the surrounding property.

This is where she lives? Alone? Impossible! Well, at least unlikely.

With whom?

He climbed back into his car and drove toward the city, mulling over what she'd said about herself. Not much. Her parents had moved from their home in the Bronx to Phoenix. Her sister was dead. Her brother lived in California.

A previous relationship? "It's all over," she'd said.

Over. She'd sounded definite enough, but still, he wondered. Had it really ended? Maybe the man was away on some trip and that was why she'd had this evening free.

No, she was too straightforward for that, he thought, as he shifted gears and pulled onto the interstate.

Hell, what did it matter anyway?

But he knew that Cynthia Rogers did matter. And that he wanted to know all about her. He could, of course, ask Cranston. But he hated being so devious, so openly prying. Anyway, he could learn whatever he needed to know from her. For he certainly intended to see her again. And again. He smiled as he maneuvered the Jaguar into the fast lane.

SHE WOULD NOT. She could not go out with him again. Not ever.

Long after the garage door slammed, Cindy sat in the car, her hands pressed to her burning face, trying to make sense of her jumbled emotions. She'd begun to feel so comfortable with him.

And then he had touched her. Hardly at all. His lips had merely brushed hers for one brief moment. Ever so slightly. And she had been shaken to the roots, ready to throw herself into his arms.

Oh, Lord, maybe she was...love-starved! It was so long since she'd been kissed. Her giggle was almost a sob. It was so long.

Come on, Cindy! No man's kiss, not even Dan's, had ever affected her like this. And Clay Kencade of all people, well-known for his many short-term affairs. Rich. Powerful. *Quite out of your class, Cindy.*

But tonight, in his apartment, he'd seemed almost like the boy next door. Like an old friend. He had cooked for her, made her feel relaxed and comfortable. Oh, she'd been afraid to go up to his place at first. Afraid he might make a pass.

Good thing he hadn't. Because if he'd touched her, she might have seduced *him*! Her first instinct had been right. Run.

But why? she asked herself as she finally opened the door and got out of the car. Why should she run from him, from these feelings? How did that song go? Something about the heart afraid of breaking that never learns to dance?

She could dance with Clay Kencade, laugh with him, walk arm in arm. Enjoy the moment, however brief. She was in a euphoric mood as she entered the silent house. It could be wonderful.

She tapped at Mrs. Stewart's door to let her know she was back. Then, as she mounted the stairs, her thoughts took an abrupt turn.

The children. How could she have forgotten? Any man she became involved with would of necessity become involved with them. Like Dan. She simply could not afford to take any risks that might jeopardize their happiness.

Anyway, why was she making such a big deal out of one evening? He might not even ask her out again. And if he did, she would refuse.

In Teri's room, Cindy loosened the child's grip on her teddy bear and arranged her in a more comfortable position. She took two trucks and a fire engine out of Jamey's bed and turned off the bedside lamp. Johnny's television was blinking silently and she flipped it off. Little devil, he knew he wasn't supposed to have it on, she thought as she dropped a kiss on his forehead. Then she went to her own room and to bed.

She did not dream about Clay Kencade.

TWO WEEKS LATER, Clay Kencade looked across his desk and spoke to his architect. "The tenants have received their notice and some have already vacated."

"Good. Now, as soon as you decide on the anchor store, I'll get started on the first draft. I think everything can be contained in the area we have."

"I think so, too. If I expanded any further, I'd be displacing my customers."

"Right. And what's a shopping mall without customers? I'll be in touch," the architect added as he departed.

Clay sat for a moment feeling nostalgic and a bit melancholy as he thought of tearing down the old four-story building he had inherited from his father. It was the largest building in the two-block area he'd acquired for his new shopping center. Some apartments, but mostly small business units. Funny how some things never changed. The coin laundry that had helped pay his college fees was still in operation.

The neighborhood was beginning to look a little dilapidated, though. A bit run-down, but still occupied mainly by solidly middle-class families, many of them professors or students from the nearby university. Maybe he'd buy a few of the brownstones, fix them up a bit without removing the tenants. Give the whole area a face-lift, more in keeping with the proposed shopping mall. He felt excited, as he always did when he started a new project. Already he could picture the shoppers strolling through his new center, among vibrant green trees and restful fountains.

He stood up, walked to the window and looked down at the avenue traffic, miniature cars crawling along. A light rain had started, and he watched umbrellas popping up like tiny colored balloons as people poured from the surrounding buildings. Going home. Or somewhere. Cynthia Rogers would be among them.

His hand tightened on the keys in his pocket. He didn't understand her. He really didn't. And it bothered him that he was bothered. But why the devil did she refuse every invitation he issued? That night in his apartment had been special. They had talked and laughed and— Maybe it hadn't been special to her. Maybe she would have preferred the Ritz.

Well, hell, if that was what she wanted... But she never gave him a chance. Every time he approached her, she forestalled him. "I'm sorry.... Another appointment... It's just that I'm so busy these days.... I really don't have the time."

Why the hell not? What took up her time in that big house in Greenwich? *Who* was probably more to the point!

"All right, Mr. K. Friday afternoon wrap-up."

He smiled at Maggie as she took her seat beside his desk and produced the inevitable notebook.

"Let's see," she said. "You have the Sanderses' cocktail party tomorrow night and the theater afterward."

"Cancel it."

"Check. Golf—the usual foursome Sunday morning at seven and—" The phone rang and she picked it up. "Oh, good afternoon, Mrs. Daniels. How are you?" She looked at Clay. He shook his head. "Oh, I'm so sorry. He's already left for the day. Could I give him a message? No, I'm not sure where he can be reached. I know he had a late appointment." Maggie said goodbye and looked up at him. "She wants you to call. Urgent." He shrugged and she continued, "Now let's see...." She went on listing his appointments.

Clay, only half listening, walked around and sat at his desk, opened a drawer and propped his foot on it. "You know, Maggie, I think I made a mistake."

"Oh?" She didn't look up.

"I took this lady to my apartment."

"But you never—" This time she did look up in surprise. "I mean, you always say you have a hard enough time when they start tracking you to the office and that you'd never take a lady to your apartment. As a matter of fact, you've told me not to give out the phone number or the address."

"I know. I know. But this one's not a tracker." He rubbed his nose. "I guess she's more in the class of an... er... an evader."

"Evader?"

"Well, she manages to evade me anyway."

"Oh-ho! Quite a challenge, huh? To the sought-after Clay Kencade!"

"Cut it out, Maggie! So what's on for Monday?"

She focused on his calendar again, while he wondered if she was right. A challenge? But why did he have this sinking feeling whenever he remembered that soon he would no longer see Cynthia Rogers striding through the lobby? The damn audit was almost over and Cranston was back.

"Oh, yes," said Maggie. "Sam Alexander called twice. He's anxious to see you. Four o'clock Monday is still open. Do you want to squeeze him in?"

Sam Alexander. Clay smiled, remembering Ms Cynthia Rogers trying to tell him, while being careful *not* to tell him, that the man was a dirty crook.

"Mr. K.?"

"No. Let him know I've changed my mind. I'm not interested. I've done a little investigating. But it's not necessary to tell him that." He sat up. Sam Alexander! That was as good an excuse as any.

CYNTHIA STOOD in the driveway, holding fast to the bike, and frowned at Johnny. "You're not going anywhere, young man. Not until you've pulled every one of those weeds!" It shouldn't take long; the flower bed was small.

"I am too going! You can't stop me." He tugged at the handlebars, and it was all she could do to keep her balance. "I'm just going down to Todd's 'cause his dad's going to play catch with us. I can pull 'em when I come back."

"That's what you said last week and I let you go and you didn't! And you've had all week and it's not done yet!" She was torn. She knew how much he wanted to go but . . . Oh, it wasn't the weeds that mattered. He had to learn to be responsible. She'd given him a week to do the chore, reminded him constantly and it still wasn't done! She jerked at the bike, almost pulling it away. "You'd better get to the weeds if you want to go anywhere, including the game this afternoon!"

"You're mean, Cindy. Mean. My mom would let me go. She never made me pull no stinking weeds or nothing. And you're not my mother! And I'm going. So there!" He released his bike so quickly that it tumbled over, Cindy with it.

More hurt by what he'd said than by the fall, Cindy watched in dismay as he ran toward the street. Oh Lord, what if he— She saw him bump into a man who grabbed him by the shoulders.

"Hold on, buddy!" Clay Kencade turned Johnny firmly around and with one hand on his back propelled him back toward Cindy. "That's no way to talk to a lady. I think you should apologize."

Cindy stood up, dusting the back of her shorts, feeling like an idiot. Furious at Johnny. Furious that Kencade had witnessed the scene. Furious. Embarrassed. Helpless.

Kencade wasn't looking at her. He bent toward Johnny. "I didn't hear that apology."

"Sorry."

"That's better." Kencade, ignoring the fact that Johnny neither looked nor sounded sorry, reached out a hand. "I'm Clay Kencade. What's your name?"

"Johnny. Johnny Atwood." He reluctantly took Kencade's hand, but his face smoldered with belligerence at this stranger who had taken control.

Cynthia was also confused, albeit relieved. What would she have done if Johnny really had run defiantly off? Now, not sure what to do next, she gestured toward the flower bed. "The weeds are still there."

Johnny frowned, but Kencade spoke quickly. "You know something? It always takes less time to do a task than it does to argue yourself out of it. Would you like to make a bet on that?"

"A bet?"

Kencade walked over to the flower bed while Johnny stared at him uncertainly. "I bet we could clear out these weeds in twenty . . . no, half an hour. If I'm right, maybe there'll still be time and Cynthia will permit you to go play with your friend." He glanced at Cindy and she nodded. "Okay? Now, if it takes longer, then I lose and I'll have to play a little catch with you. Okay?"

For a moment she thought Johnny might refuse. He was just as stubborn as his dad had been! She held her breath while she waited for his answer.

"Okay." Johnny joined Kencade, who made a little ritual of checking his watch. Then they started to work.

Cindy watched them, her irritation and relief tinged with bewilderment. He had just walked up her driveway, uninvited. He'd witnessed a disgraceful spat and had taken charge. He hadn't even spoken to her—not even hello. Now there he was, talking with Johnny and pulling weeds, as unmindful of his designer jeans as he had been of his silk shirt the night he'd cooked dinner. He was so—

Oh, good heavens! She'd better check on Jamey and Teri. Quickly she stepped over Johnny's mitt and around the fallen bike and ran into the house.

She needn't have worried. Still in their pajamas, they sat on the floor, transfixed by the TV screen. Cindy scooted Teri back a bit. "You're sitting too close, pumpkin. Now, as soon as that cartoon's over, we'll go upstairs for your baths. We're going to Johnny's game after lunch, so we'll have to be ready."

She rinsed and stacked the cereal bowls, wiped the kitchen counter, then took the two children up to dress. All the while, she was extremely conscious of Clay Kencade. She could not still the sensations stirring in the pit of her stomach, could not banish from her mind the tall muscular figure standing in her flower bed. Indeed, as she dressed the children she could hear him chatting with Johnny and was irked that she couldn't discern what they said

She was buttoning Teri's sundress when Johnny came up.

"I'm done," he proudly announced—a pride rather at odds with his former resistance, Cindy observed.

"You're *finished*. Cakes get done."

"I mean I'm finished. In twenty-nine minutes. Can I go over to Todd's now?"

"You *may* go. For one hour. Wait!" she called as he started out. "Where's Mr. Kencade?"

"His name is Clay. Downstairs. Waiting to see you," he shouted as he bounded down.

She tried to repress an unwelcome surge of excitement as she walked slowly downstairs, Teri in her arms and Jamey racing ahead. Kencade was sitting at the game table, but when they came in he stood up, his surprise so evident that Cynthia felt her face burn. Like the old woman who lived in the shoe . . .

"Hi!" Jamey skidded to a stop in front of Clay, who crouched in front of him.

"Hello. Who're you?"

"I'm Jamey. Are you going to marry Cindy?"

"Well, I . . . er . . ." He got to his feet, darting a quick glance at Cindy.

"Dan was going to. Only he didn't. Dan has a boat and he took us sailing. Do you have a boat?"

"Jamey!" Cindy rushed forward, wishing she could muzzle the boy. Or hide her face as Teri was doing against Cindy's neck. "It's not polite to bombard a guest with questions. This is Mr. Kencade. Say hello to him."

"I did already say hi, didn't I?"

"Indeed you did," Kencade assured him, a glint of amusement in his eyes. "And who is this young lady?" He pulled aside one of Teri's curls and looked at her. She stared silently back, her arms tightening around Cindy's neck.

"That's Teri. She's the baby and she—"

"Teri, say hello to Mr. Kencade," Cindy urged, attempting to drown out whatever information Jamey was ready to impart. "It takes time for her to become acquainted. When she gets used to you she'll talk quite enough." Darn! Why did she say that? She didn't want her to get used to him.

She hustled the two children outside as soon as she could, telling them not to play in the sandbox, so they'd still be clean when it was time to go. Then she turned to Kencade, assuring herself that he couldn't possibly hear the wild pounding of her heart.

"Could I fix you something cold to drink? Soda, iced tea or—or something stronger?"

"Iced tea would be great." He followed her into the kitchen and sat on one of the bar stools.

How does he always manage to look so much at ease when I feel so uncomfortable and awkward? she thought, as she took down a pitcher and began to mix the instant tea. Conscious of his eyes on her, she spoke before she could think. "Why are you looking at me like that?"

"I just can't believe that you look even younger than when I first saw you. You seem more like a slightly older sister than . . . what are you? An aunt?"

She nodded and reached for two glasses.

"Have I met them all?"

"All?" She'd been putting the ice into the glasses, but now she stopped to give him a puzzled stare.

"All the children."

"Oh. Yes, of course." She poured tea into the glasses.

"Claire's?"

"Yes."

"You didn't mention them."

"Oh. Didn't I? Wait, I'll get some mint." She hurried out, glanced to see that the children were okay and plucked two sprigs of mint from the patch beside the patio. She went back in, rinsed the mint and tucked a sprig in each glass, then handed one to him. "We'd better go outside so I can watch them."

"Why didn't you?" he asked when they were seated at the table on the patio.

"Why didn't I what?"

"Mention the children."

"Oh. Guess I didn't think about them." She blushed as she noted the elaborate, very doubtful lift of his eyebrow. She turned away, looking in the children's direction, and saw Teri heading for the sandbox. "No, Teri. Don't play in the sand. Play ball with her, Jamey. I don't want her all dirty."

"She can't throw," Jamey protested.

"Well, push her on the swing then." Cindy walked over to the children and lifted Teri into one of the swings. "There. Jamey's going to push you. Please, Jamey. Not too high now," she warned as Jamey began to push and she returned to the patio.

"Life gets rough sometimes, huh?" She was surprised at the understanding in Kencade's voice.

He reached over and took her hand, sending a warm ripple through her—as though a magnet were pulling her closer to him. His thumb gently caressed the back of her hand and she saw that he was staring at the nail she had bitten. Embarrassed, she pulled her hand away, took a sip of tea.

"I forgot to thank you," she said. "And not just for pulling weeds." She tried to laugh. It seemed such a ridiculous task for Clay Kencade. "For the way you handled Johnny. Sometimes I...oh, I don't know. Anyway, you disciplined him, you made him do the job, without belittling him. Thank you."

He grinned. "My second stepfather had a nine-year-old brat. I was only a couple of years older, but I had to learn to handle him in self-defense."

"You must have had loads of experience," she said slowly. All those stepfathers, the different homes.

"Wide and varied," he agreed wryly.

"You've certainly had more experience than I have," she said. "I confess I didn't know what to do. If you hadn't come along..." Her voice trailed off and there was a definite question in her eyes. He stirred uneasily, then remembered he had an excuse for showing up unannounced at her door.

"I wanted to ask you about something," he said. "The other night you mentioned a man—Sam Alexander."

"Oh?" A flush stole across her face and she looked wary.

"I'd like some inside data on his Aloha Paper Company."

"Inside data?" The emphasis was on the first word and he sensed her withdrawal.

He felt a little guilty. He shouldn't be making her uncomfortable when he'd already done the investigating and come to his own decision. Still, he couldn't resist adding, "Carruthers and Cranston are the accountants of record."

"Well, now those records are at court, so they're available to any eligible and interested party."

"Cynthia, you and I both know that figures can lie." He looked directly at her. "When I deal with a man in business I like to know more about him than the color of his eyes. And you did say—"

"That I didn't like the look in Sam Alexander's eyes." She smiled. "And that, Clay Kencade, is all you're going to get from me. Would you like another glass of tea?"

He nodded and watched her fill his glass again. She might look young, but she was a real professional. No matter what she thought of a person, no matter how much she knew, she would not betray a client's confidentiality. He liked that. He even liked the good-natured way she'd told him to back off.

Cynthia wondered if he planned to do more investigating. She hoped so. Clay seemed to be a straightforward kind of guy, and she'd hate to see him get involved with Sam Alexander.

"I'm home, Cindy. Just like I promised." She heard Johnny's bike slam into the garage, then saw him come running around to the patio. "Back in one hour like you said."

"Good, Johnny. Now stay out here with Teri while I fix lunch. I have to hurry," she said to Kencade.

"I thought you couldn't cook," he said.

"No, but I'm an expert with peanut butter and jelly. Please excuse me."

He didn't leave. She couldn't believe it. There he sat at the kitchen table, munching peanut butter sandwiches, helping Teri with her milk and discussing the tooth fairy with Jamey. Jamey was a believer. In everything. Santa Claus, the tooth fairy, the Easter bunny. Cindy marveled that Clay Kencade understood this. Probably one of his stepfathers had had a five-year-old.

Cindy felt as if she were in a dream and had to force herself to move briskly and efficiently, for otherwise they'd never be ready on time. When lunch was over she had to help Johnny look for his uniform, which they finally found on the dryer where Mrs. Stewart had left it. Then she had to change. She felt rather silly when she came down in the baseball uniform Steve Prescott had ordered for her. But all she saw in Kencade's eyes was a glint of appreciation.

"You amaze me, Cynthia Rogers. A woman of many facets. What talents will you display next?" Then to Johnny's whooping delight he offered him a ride in the Jaguar. "I'll take you to the game. I'd like to see you and your coach in action," he said, his mouth twisting in a charming crooked smile.

Doesn't he have anywhere else to go? Cindy thought, trying to concentrate on her driving and not on the man driving behind her. He ought to be going to some meeting or hopping on a plane, trying to get somewhere before someone else. All the big financiers she'd ever heard of— like Donald Trump and that Japanese guy who said he never took off his running shoes—were always in a rush. Not Clay Kencade! He had time to cook and pull weeds and sit around talking about the tooth fairy. When he ought to be busy trying to beat the competition—or at least find out about people like Sam Alexander.

A moment later they reached the field and Cindy put all thoughts of business from her mind. Ginger, the coach's little girl, took charge of Teri and Jamey, while Cindy and Johnny hurried to the dugout. She had time for only a brief nod to Clay Kencade, who settled in the bleachers to watch.

After only two innings the game was turning into a disaster. The Semco Cubs were clearly outclassed by the well-trained Pizza Pirates and their expert pitcher. Cindy tried to give her full attention to the game, but couldn't help glancing toward the bleachers every few minutes. At Clay Kencade.

Cindy was concerned when Johnny, after his second strikeout, threw down his bat and ran off crying. She saw Kencade come down to talk to him. But she didn't have time to watch. She was coaching Todd, their best batter, who'd managed to steal third base. Davey Prescott, next up at bat, bunted, and Cindy yelled, "Now, Todd! Run!" He slid in to score.

The next time she looked toward the bleachers, Kencade was gone. She tried to deny a certain lowering of her spirits, swallowed and turned back to the game. They lost, 27 to 7. A complete disaster.

Johnny looked despondent as they climbed back into the station wagon. Cindy complimented him on the catch he had made out in right field. "It's just as important to put a man out, you know, as it is to make a home run." She did not ask when Clay Kencade had left. She wouldn't think about him.

Only later, when the children were in bed and she was alone, did her emotions melt her resolve. She could think of nothing or no one else. She sat up in bed, her fingers between the pages of the novel that could not hold her attention, and basked in the memory of the day.

It had seemed so natural to have him here. His presence had been almost soothing.

Soothing, Cindy?

Her face burned as she remembered the magnetic pull she'd felt when he touched her. She remembered how her hand had begun to tingle. Now she looked down at her thumb and immediately tucked it under her fingers. She must stop biting her nails!

"Cindy?" It was almost a whisper, accompanied by a soft knock on her door.

"Johnny?"

He pushed open the door and walked in slowly. He stood beside the bed in his rumpled pajamas, tearstains evident on his face.

"I'm sorry, Cindy."

"Oh, honey, it's all right. You already said—"

"I mean about saying you weren't my mom," he gulped. "I know you're not, but I didn't mean to..." He couldn't get the words out.

"Oh, Johnny, come here." She pulled him up onto the bed, holding him close, with his back against her. "I understand. You miss your mother, don't you?" He nodded and she felt sobs rack the little body. She just held him for a while and let him cry. It wasn't true that children quickly forget. She had to remember that he wasn't still a baby like Teri and Jamey, that for him the memories were more painful.

"I know how you feel," she said when his sobs subsided a bit. She rubbed her chin on his soft hair. "I miss your mom, too, you know. When you love someone and they're gone, you can't help but miss them."

"Yeah. I miss Dad, too. And Dan." He looked up at her. "Why did you send Dan away, Cindy?"

"I..." She stopped. Would it hurt more to know that it was Dan who had deserted? "It's just that—well, people get busy. Dan is a lawyer and has lots of people making demands on him. And I have a busy job and there just wasn't the time to spend with each other. But—" she hugged the boy a little tighter "—we'll always have time for each other, won't we?"

He nodded. "I—I'm sorry I yelled at you, Cindy."

"I know. I understand about that, too." She tried to laugh. "I bet we'll have many more bouts like we had today. Because I care about you and I'll always be telling you what to do. We shouldn't get upset and yell at each other. But if we do...well, we'll always work things out because we know we love each other."

"Oh, Cindy, I do love you."

"And I love you and we're going to try not to yell at each other. Okay?" She talked until he was calm, then led the way to another topic. Baseball. Perhaps not the best choice.

"I wasn't very good today, was I?"

"Oh, honey, you can't expect to be perfect right away. It takes practice."

"That's just what Clay said."

"He did?"

"Yep. He said even Joe Samuels didn't start out batting four hundred."

"Who's Joe Samuels?"

"Cindy! He's tops. The very best batter in the National League. But Clay says he had to practice and practice before he got to be the best. And Clay says he's going to come out and pitch some balls to me."

"Oh." She felt a prickle of apprehension but hastened to say, "Well, that's...good. You know he's a very busy man, though, and he might not always have the time."

"But he said he would. He promised!" Johnny's face was alight with a belief that she hadn't the heart to destroy.

But after she'd taken him back to his own room and tucked him in, she remembered his saying he missed Dan. Children didn't understand. They expected more than some people were willing or able to give. And when a person made promises and then didn't follow through, they were hurt.

It was safer not to get too close.

CHAPTER FIVE

"GUESS WHAT, CINDY!" Johnny greeted her when she arrived home Monday evening. "Clay came out this afternoon and pitched balls to me."

"And I catched them," said Jamey.

"Caught them," Cindy automatically corrected as she ruffled Jamey's hair.

"He did not!" Johnny declared. "He just kept getting in the way and Clay kept telling him to stay out of range!"

"But when they rolled on the ground I catched—caught them. And I put them back in the bucket for Clay to throw again."

"Me too!" Teri said as she rushed to Cindy with arms outstretched.

"My, you had an exciting afternoon." Cindy scooped up Teri and gave her a hug, while trying to adjust to the idea of Clay Kencade taking an afternoon off to pitch balls to a nine-year-old kid. She hadn't expected it. She put the little girl down and went in to greet Mrs. Stewart. "How was your day?" she asked.

"Just fine." The housekeeper was peering into the oven. "We had a visitor this afternoon." She took out a savory roast and set it on the tiled counter. Then she called to the boys, "Go and wash, kids. Dinner's ready. Johnny, take care of Teri and don't forget to use soap." She turned back to Cindy. "A Mr. Kencade. He came here with a bucket of balls just after Johnny got home from school. He said he was out this way on some business and Johnny explained that he'd visited you on Saturday and arranged to practice with him." Mrs. Stewart looked a little anxious. "It's all right? You don't mind, do you?"

"Of course not," said Cindy. Did she mind? In a way, she was glad he hadn't disappointed Johnny. Yet she was hoping he wouldn't make these visits a habit. Johnny would begin to expect too much. Dan had played with the children and he—

Oh, she should stop worrying. And she should stop thinking about Clay Kencade!

But that was easier said than done. All through dinner, homework and bedtime stories, she kept remembering Clay's quick engaging smile, that way he had of taking charge, the way he'd handled Johnny's little rebellion about the weeding by making a game out of work. And this afternoon. Maybe he *had* just been in the area. Still, it was kind of him to remember Johnny, to bring the balls and take the time.

Even after the children were in bed and she was seated at her bedroom desk, her mind kept drifting back to Clay. Perhaps, she thought with a chuckle, it was easier to think about a handsome man than to concentrate on what she was supposed to be doing—the monthly bills, the chore she hated most of all. It always made her nervous to write out that stack of checks and watch her bank account diminish.

She picked up the envelope from the gas company and hesitated, gnawing on her thumbnail. Last month's heating bill had been monstrous. But this time it wasn't too bad. Thank goodness for an early spring! And it would be still less as summer progressed. The house was well insulated and with those high ceilings they seldom needed air-conditioning.

A notice from the school indicated that tuition would be increased next fall. Cindy sighed. She would hate to take the kids out of the school. Claire had been so pleased with the instruction they received there.

Claire. Cindy's eyes misted. Claire had been disappointed in so many things—her husband, her own life cut short, so little time to enjoy her children. Somehow Cindy hated to disrupt any routine that Claire had started and—

The phone rang.

It was Marcy Prescott. After a cheerful greeting she asked Cindy if she had a list of the scheduled games for the Semco Cubs. "And the names and addresses of the parents," she added. "I'm supposed to make arrangements for which parent is to bring treats for which game. Honestly, Steve expects me to be as efficient as his secretaries, but then he flies off to Texas with all the Little League stuff in his briefcase! At least, I guess that's where it is. I can't find it anywhere."

Cindy joined in her good-natured laughter and said her lists were in her desk at the office. She would send copies to Marcy.

"Hey!" said Marcy. "I've got a better idea. I'm coming into town tomorrow. Why don't I pick them up? We could meet for lunch."

Cindy said she'd like that, and they arranged to meet at the Classic at twelve-thirty.

So the next morning when Cindy received a call from Clay Kencade inviting her to lunch, she had to refuse. "I'm sorry," she told him. And she really was. He'd been so kind to Johnny; she wanted him to know how much she appreciated that. "Thank you for coming out to practice with Johnny. He was just thrilled."

"I enjoyed it," he said. "Sorry you're engaged. Perhaps another time?"

"Of course. Give me a call anytime." Cindy hung up, chiding herself for feeling disappointed. Hadn't she decided it was best not to get involved with Clay Kencade? And she was looking forward to meeting Marcy Prescott for lunch. Although they didn't know each other very well yet, Cindy sensed that they could become good friends. She liked Marcy.

She liked her even more as their lunch progressed. Marcy looked stunningly chic in her navy-blue maternity dress, but what caught your attention, Cindy decided, was her warm genial smile, the sparkle in her eyes, her buoyant air. Marcy Prescott was obviously a happy woman. As soon as they were seated she took a box from her overloaded shopping bag and opened it.

"I came into town to pick up some necessities—sleepers and things—but I couldn't resist this," she said, holding up a frilly pink baby's dress.

"Oh, it's darling!" Cindy cried. "With those tiny pleats and that lace collar! I can see why you couldn't resist."

"And I'm glad we met for lunch. I couldn't wait to show it off."

"So you know you're having a girl?"

"Yes. I've had all the tests." She put the dress away and they gave the waitress their orders.

"Are the children happy about the baby?" Cindy asked.

"Oh, yes. Ginger, who wanted a girl, is beside herself. Davey wanted a boy, but he's being very philosophical about it. He says the baby won't be big enough to play baseball anyway."

"And Steve?"

"Just as happy about a girl as he would be about a boy, since, as he says, we already have one of each. But he's driving me crazy trying to make sure the baby and I are both healthy. Would you believe..." Marcy laughed as she dug into her salad and launched into a series of anecdotes about how "ridiculously protective" Steve had become. Cindy noticed that Marcy's face took on a special glow when she talked about her husband.

They're really in love, she thought. And they must have been married for at least ten years, because Davey was nine. But Marcy looked as if she was still on her honeymoon. Cindy felt a trace of envy. Would it have been that way if she'd married Dan? But as she listened to Marcy, Cindy knew she hadn't loved Dan. Not really, not with that kind of depth. Anyway, even love didn't always last. Claire's marriage had deteriorated more with the birth of each child. Cindy pushed the thought of Claire from her mind and resolutely concentrated on what Marcy was saying.

"Steve tells me you're an honest-to-goodness C.P.A.! I'm impressed." Marcy's eyes were wide with admiration. "I can't even balance my checkbook."

Cindy laughed and said that dealing with figures was much easier than dealing with children. And the talk reverted to the problems of parenting.

It was a pleasant lunch, and as they parted, Cindy was glad to hear Marcy say, "I've really enjoyed this. Let's meet again soon."

"Yes, let's," Cindy agreed warmly. She felt a satisfaction, a lightness of spirit, at the rapport and the understanding between them. She'd been right—Marcy Prescott was going to be a special friend.

WHEN CLAY REACHED his flat late that evening, the phone was ringing. An unusual occurrence, since so few people had that number. He lifted the receiver from the bedside table. It was Clarice, the youngest of his stepsisters.

"Clay," she said, "I thought you liked Julie!"

"Julie?" Clay sat on his bed, loosening his tie, and tried to place the name.

"My friend, Julie Compton. You met her at one of George's district parties. And I brought her with me that day I had lunch with you at the Classic. Remember?"

"Oh, yes." The little dark-haired schoolteacher.

"She tells me she hasn't seen you since you took her to that play."

Now he remembered. He'd felt a little sorry for Julie because she had said she loved plays but seldom got to see any of the new ones. And Clarice had mentioned that Clay had season tickets to several of the drama series. So he'd arranged a theater and dinner date with Julie. The play had been quite entertaining. Julie? Sweet and pleasant, but—there was no other word for it—boring.

"I thought you liked her!" Clarice said again.

"I do. She's nice."

"Nice! Is that all you can say about her? You know what your problem is, Clay? You've got so many of those sleek career women chasing you that you can't recognize the real thing when you see it! Julie is such a sweet delightful person. If you'd give yourself a chance to really know her—"

"Now, Clarice," he broke in, recognizing that she was about to start her usual you-need-to-settle-down line, "you know how busy I am."

"Men!" she scoffed. "You sound just like George when he's trying to avoid something. Anyway, what I called about is this barbecue we're having. It's a whole month away, so you can just fit it into your calendar right now!"

They chatted a few minutes longer, and he hung up after promising to come to the barbecue at their Long Island home. Of course she would have Julie Compton there. Clarice was the most possessive of the sisters and a determined arranger of other people's lives. Too bad she was the one who lived closest to him. Or maybe not. Her husband, George Edwards, had turned out to be his best district manager, and it was Clarice who had talked him into hiring George.

But you're not talking me into marriage, little sister, and certainly not to anyone like Julie, he thought as he flung his coat and tie onto the bed.

He went into the kitchen, poured himself a brandy and sipped it. Cynthia Rogers was certainly a busy lady. But then, she had to be with a full-time job and those kids, even coaching a baseball team. He chuckled. She did look cute in that baseball outfit!

Still, why did it have to be all work and no play except with the children? No time, even for lunch. Very soon now the audit would be finished, and she wouldn't even be coming to the building anymore.

But if she worked for him . . .

CYNTHIA WAS SURPRISED when Kencade came into the accounting section two days in a row. She was always keenly aware of his presence, always affected by it. But what really made her nervous was his inordinate interest in what she was doing. He bent over her desk, looking at her screen and her ledgers, and asked numerous questions, many of them quite irrelevant to the audit. On Thursday he didn't come down but she received a phone call from him.

"There's a problem we need to discuss, Cynthia." His tone was brisk and businesslike. "Would you be free for a lunch meeting? Say Conway's at twelve-thirty?"

"Why, yes. Of course." What problem? As far as she knew everything was going smoothly. Anyway, whatever it was should be discussed with Cranston. She expected to see her boss at the meeting, but wondered if she should call him first. Finally, Cindy decided she'd probably been included because she was in charge of the audit for this quarter; that seemed a reasonable enough assumption.

"Mr. Kencade's table?" said the hostess. "Right this way, please."

Kencade stood to greet her at a table obviously meant for two. She hesitated, not sitting in the chair he pulled out for her.

"Where's Cranston?" she asked.

"Cranston?"

"I was sure he'd be here. You said there was a problem about the audit."

He smiled. "No. Sit down, Cynthia." She did so and he returned to his chair. "No problem with the audit."

"But you said—"

"That I had a problem I wished to discuss with you."

"Oh." She was glad she hadn't called Cranston, after all. But what was this about?

"Will you have something from the bar, Mr. Kencade?" asked the waiter.

"Cynthia?"

"Er...white wine, please." She felt confused and somehow that she'd been tricked. He had said a meeting and naturally she'd thought—

"The usual for me, Porter," Kencade said to the waiter. "All right," he began as the man retreated. "I can see you're puzzled, so I'm not going to beat around the bush. How would you like to work for me?"

"Work for you?" she repeated, feeling even more confused. He had a floor full of accountants. "Doing what?"

"Acquisition analyst. You could check those figures to which I'm so allergic and you're so attracted—and advise me."

"But—" This was totally unexpected. "I thought...that is, Mr. Morrison—"

"Tom's overloaded. And to tell you the truth, I think he's as allergic to new projects as I am to figures."

"He probably thinks you're taking on too many. So do I." She was on firmer ground now. She'd been longing to tell him that he was expanding too rapidly. "In just one year, your acquisitions have jumped—" She broke off as the waiter reappeared with their drinks and paused to receive their orders. The conversation then turned to favorite foods and restaurants, and Cindy felt relieved that she'd been interrupted and the subject changed. For goodness' sake, she scolded herself, a man approaches you with a job offer and right away you start telling him how to run his business. Even before you tell him you're *not* going to take the job.

"You were starting to say something about the extent of my acquisitions," Clay prompted when their salads had been set before them.

"And I was quite out of line."

"Come on, Cindy! Say what you think! That's why I want to hire you. That's the kind of input I need." He put down his fork. "Frankly, I've been very impressed with you. To begin with, you're quick. The first day you came into my office you analyzed data in ten minutes that some accountants would sputter over for two hours."

"You make me sound like a walking profit and loss sheet."

"Those come a dime a dozen. More to the point, you explain the sheets so they make sense to me. You're more than a bean counter." He leaned forward, both arms resting on the table. She could tell he was serious. "You have the kind of comprehensive overall vision I need."

Now she understood why he had hovered over her work, asking all those seemingly irrelevant questions. She couldn't help feeling a glow of pride. All the same, she couldn't possibly accept.

"I thank you for your confidence in me, and for the offer," she said carefully. "But..." She paused, arrested by the intimacy of his smile and conscious of the responsive warmth stealing through her. "I do appreciate the offer but I must decline. I'm quite happy where I am."

"Are you saying that I made a mistake?"

"Mistake?"

"In assessing your qualifications. If you're in the habit of making a decision before considering all the details then you don't belong in my organization."

That nettled. "I don't see why not. That seems to be the way *you* operate."

His eyebrow went up and he chuckled. "Okay. Point taken. But that's the aspect I'm trying to correct. If you come to work for me..." He fell silent as if a thought had just occurred to him. "Are you under a long-term contract with Carruthers and Cranston, or did you sign an agreement not to take on any of their clients?"

She shook her head.

He folded his arms and regarded her solemnly. "Then why don't you want to work for me?"

Because when you look at me like that, something melts inside me and I feel dizzy and confused and I don't want to get involved and I don't want the children hurt. She wanted to throw up her hands and tell him to leave her alone. Instead, she pushed aside her salad, straightened her shoulders and spoke frankly, determined to tell the truth or at least part of it. "Look, Mr. Kencade, it's just that right now I have a lot of responsibility. The children... well, I'm just starting to get a handle on things.

And at least my job is routine. I'm just not prepared to take on any changes."

"Yes. I can understand that. I know how you feel." There was such concern in his voice and such discernment in his dark eyes that she felt herself blush. "Still, I don't see how a job only a few blocks from where you work right now would change anything," he said in a reasonable voice. "And the hours might be even better. You'd probably be able to do some of your work from home. It wouldn't be necessary for you to travel from office to office the way you do now. And the salary...of course I'm not aware of your present salary. But you'd have a great deal of responsibility here, and..." He thought for a moment, then mentioned a sum that made her gasp. It was almost twice as much as she was currently making.

Braces. Tuition. Dancing lessons for Teri. Oh, how the money would lessen the strain. Vacations might even be possible.

She smiled and couldn't help saying, "If I worked for you I think my first suggestion would be that you cut salaries."

He laughed. "You get what you pay for. I have an excellent staff. You'd earn your money. Now, listen to this." He went on, listing the advantages for both of them if she joined Kencade Enterprises.

Cindy was tempted. It was a job that would really interest her and one she could handle. More important, she knew she would be of benefit to Kencade Enterprises. And the salary...

But she would be working closely with Clay Kencade. Every day, she would experience that little glow of excitement she felt now as she watched him, full of anticipation as he talked of future ventures. She would be swept along in the dynamic force that emanated from him and made her feel exhilarated, challenged, and so alive!

Yet she remembered the last time she'd been caught by a force. Dan. She always insisted that she didn't miss him. And it was true she hadn't been as deeply in love with him as she'd once thought. But there was no denying that his going had left a gap in her life.

She knew with a dreadful certainty that any gap left by Clay Kencade would be unbearable. She could not take the risk.

"No," she said. "I really do appreciate your offer, but I'd rather not make a change right now."

"I understand. But don't slam the door." His manner seemed conciliatory, although she could tell he was non-plussed. This man was not accustomed to refusals. "Why don't you come up to my office—say at the close of business on Monday and we'll talk some more. It wouldn't be too much of a change, you know. Think it over during the weekend."

"If you insist." But she'd made her decision. There was no need to give it any further thought.

Yet she did think about it during the days that followed. Constantly, no matter what she was doing—serving pizza to the kids, coaching the baseball team, bathing Teri—the job offer was foremost in her mind.

The work itself. It would be so exciting.

The pay. Was she wrong to turn down that kind of money? It could make things so easy. No worry about the increased tuition. She could put Teri in nursery school. No fretting over the monthly bills.

And what made her think their involvement would be a personal one? Kencade was a busy man—at play as well as work. If the tabloids were right about all his ladies and his love life, he would hardly consider her a prize, she thought with some amusement. All she had to do was keep her cool. Keep everything businesslike.

Well . . . why not?

Monday afternoon she found it hard to concentrate on the figures on her computer screen, hard to ignore the little sparks of anticipation that nudged at her. She told herself to calm down. All she had to do was accept the offer and discuss the terms in a businesslike manner.

If he suggested dinner or drinks to celebrate . . . Oh, for goodness' sake, why did she think he would? And if he did, she could just refuse. Strictly business.

But by the time she stepped into the elevator and pushed the button for the penthouse, the little sparks had flamed, had become a blaze of excited anticipation.

He wasn't there.

"He's gone for the day." Maggie, picking up her own purse, looked at Cindy with some surprise. "Did you have an appointment?"

"Yes. No. Well, that is . . . not exactly." Cindy felt a little foolish. "Anyway, it's not important," she told the secretary as they both took the elevator down to the lobby.

Not important. Cindy felt utterly deflated and she couldn't shake her disappointment. He'd acted as if her coming to work for Kencade Enterprises was so crucial to the company. And to him? *You have the kind of comprehensive overall vision I need . . .*

Well, I was right, she thought. He didn't consider her a prize—at work or play! Maybe the job offer was just a whim. He'd thought it over and changed his mind. Or forgotten all about it.

AT THE MOMENT Clay *had* forgotten. He was standing outside the Emergency Room at County Hospital trying to console the sobbing woman in his arms. He thought she'd said her name was Denise, but he couldn't be sure. All he really knew was that she was the daughter of Daniel Salter, the man who had just died.

"A heart attack," the doctors said. "That's probably what caused the fall from the scaffold."

It was the fall that had brought Kencade to the scene. Salter was not one of his regular employees, but he often used his demolition company for small jobs. The accident had happened on a Kencade project, and Clay, notified immediately, had rushed to the hospital where he found Salter's daughter alone and quite distraught.

"I should have been there for him," she kept saying over and over.

"Nonsense. You couldn't have known," he said. But he thought he knew how she felt—as he had when his father died. He told her about that, hoping it would ease her pain. "These things happen. It's not your fault," he insisted again.

He did his best to comfort her, brought coffee and stayed with her until some of her friends arrived.

"Oh, Mr. Kencade," she crooned, squeezing his hand as he was about to depart. "You were so wonderful to stay with me. I was so...so..." Seemingly overcome, she put her hand to her mouth and closed her eyes for a moment. "It meant so much to me that you were here."

"A difficult time for all of us," he said. "I'll be in touch. In the meantime, if you need anything...anything at all—" he pressed his card into her hand "—just give me a call."

CHAPTER SIX

HIS CALL CAME almost as soon as she reached her desk the next morning.

"I'm sorry to have missed you yesterday, Cynthia. I had an emergency."

He hadn't forgotten!

"Oh, that's quite all right," she said, trying to keep her voice calm.

"No, it's not all right. I really want to talk to you. Unfortunately, my calendar is rather full today. But if you could spare a few minutes this morning... Could you come up now?"

"I ... er ... yes, of course." She tried to stifle her elation. An elation due to the job itself, she sternly decided. Once she had decided to take it, she'd begun to project herself into the role. It would be stimulating, challenging, and she was eager to begin. Last night she'd been surprised and dismayed at how let down she felt. But now... Her heart fluttered and so did her stomach.

This nervous tension was only normal for someone anticipating a career change, especially one of such magnitude, she told herself, hurrying into the ladies' room to run cold water over her wrists.

She entered his office, bracing herself as he came forward to greet her.

"Nice of you to come up," he said. Amazingly, he looked almost anxious and a little nervous himself. "Well, did you think things over during the weekend?'' he asked abruptly.

"Yes." Her hands were trembling and she thrust them into the pockets of her skirt.

"And?"

There was no need, as he put it, to "beat about the bush." "This sounds like a real opportunity," she answered simply. "I think I'd like to try it."

"Good!" There was relief, delight and something else in his face. She thought for a moment that he was going to hug her. But he just smiled and said, "I'm glad. You'll be a great addition to the staff, in more ways than one."

"I—I hope so." She was trying not to be entranced by his engagingly crooked smile. And wondering about that "more ways than one" remark. Was he anticipating more than a business relationship?

But he was suddenly very businesslike. "Sit down and we'll discuss terms." He pulled out a chair for her before going around to sit at his desk. After a short, straightforward discussion, they agreed on the terms and he said he would have a contract drawn up immediately so she could have her lawyer check it before giving notice to Cranston.

As she rose to leave, she felt very good about the whole thing. She had been making a big deal out of nothing. She had never before become personally involved with either an employer or a fellow employee. Why should it be different with Clay Kencade? She would simply distance herself. And despite those one or two occasions when he'd come to Greenwich, he certainly wouldn't have either the time or the inclination to bother with kids.

"Oh, by the way, let me know when you're ready to leave today," he said. "I'll drive you home."

"Oh?" She turned from the door.

"I promised Johnny some batting practice."

PHILIP CRANSTON WAS very nice about the move. He said it was a step up for her and wished her luck. He also told her she'd been one of their best employees and that there would always be a place in the firm for her if she wanted to return.

She worked several evenings during the next two weeks in order to clear out her desk and turn over her files. Jane seemed more excited than she was herself about the new job, and Cindy couldn't help suspecting she felt just a bit envious. She kept quoting warnings to Cindy from an article on the "dangers of office affairs."

"Oh, for Pete's sake, Jane," Cindy said, "you know I'm not the type to have an affair, either in or out of the office."

"Aha! But Clay Kencade is. According to *Personalities*, he—"

"Spare me," Cindy muttered as she hauled papers from her bottom desk drawer. "How can you stand to read that trashy magazine?"

"Because it has the inside dirt on everybody who's anybody! But you won't be reading about him." Jane's voice became soft and seductive. "You'll be standing next to him, gazing into those dreamy eyes, smelling his aftershave and counting his millions."

I don't need this, Cindy thought. She made an effort to block out her feelings and frowned at the papers, trying to decide what to throw out and what to pass on. "That's what he's hiring me for," she said. "To count his millions. And that's what I'm planning to do. Our discussions will be strictly business."

"Oh, but just listen to this," Jane said, picking up her magazine. "'Sharing the excitement and problems of a job, always having something important to talk about, can be a heavy aphrodisiac.' Heavy aphrodisiac, Cindy!

You've got to be very careful if you don't want to get burned.''

Cindy dumped a pile of papers into the wastebasket and whirled around to stare at Jane. "Can this be the same woman who advised me to put on lipstick so I could entice Clay Kencade during an interview?"

"But that was different. You weren't working for him then. Listen to this." Jane adjusted her glasses and continued to read. " 'Nothing is worse in a romantic relationship than an imbalance of power between the two parties involved. And having an affair with a person who can determine your salary, your promotion and your professional future, is a risky business'!"

"Thank you for the advice! Now if you'll just hand me that folder over there. And please understand, for the umpteenth time, I am planning no affair with Clay Kencade or anybody else!"

"Okay, okay. You needn't get so huffy. I'm just trying to tell you what a vulnerable position you're in. Now I, on the other hand... Hey, Cindy, do me a favor, will you? Tell Philip Cranston I should handle the Kencade audit from now on." When Cindy's eyebrows went up, Jane laughed. "Well, I wouldn't be exactly working for him. So my career would be under no threat. And, unlike some people, I've got nothing against short-term affairs. Will you speak to Cranston, Cindy?"

"I'll do what I can." Cindy slammed the empty drawer shut, irritated by the stab of apprehension... and jealousy? Why should she care whom he had an affair with, as long as it wasn't herself!

And she didn't need Jane's warnings. She meant to keep the relationship on a business level. She had no intention of getting personally involved or letting the children...

The children. She bit her lip. Kencade had been to Greenwich three times during the past two weeks to pitch balls to Johnny. Twice she'd been working late and hadn't been there. But the time she was home she'd felt it only polite to invite him in to share the dinner Mrs. Stewart had prepared. She had seen it then—the natural rapport he'd already established with the children. And the easy way they related to him.

He had attended one of Johnny's games but left early. Of course she suspected he would be busy with his own activities on weekends. She was glad. But then she told herself she was being overconcerned. If she distanced herself, he would never become as close to the children as Dan had been. Dan had spent whole weekends with them. It wouldn't be like that with Clay Kencade. She would make sure of it.

She'd expected Personnel to place her on the sixty-third floor in the accounting section. Instead she was given her own private office in the executive suite. It was luxuriously decorated in the same beige and rich brown tones characteristic of the other executive offices. However, on one wall was a large impressionistic painting suffused with splashes of soft coral, a shade that was repeated in her leather desk chair. The accents of warm color gave the room a distinctive feminine touch, as if they had been added just for her. From the first moment she saw her office, she was completely delighted with it.

But she found it disturbing to be right around the corner from Clay's office. For one thing, she was beginning to believe the tabloids were right. She'd worked in quite a few companies during her career with Carruthers and Cranston, and never before had she seen so many women flow through the portals of one man's office. Consultants, lawyers, social as well as business associates and, of course, executives and secretaries of Kencade Enterprises. All sleek, attractive, exquisitely well groomed, and all, Cindy divined, seeking any excuse to be in the company of Clay Kencade. It really irritated her, though she didn't know why. Clay didn't seem to mind; in fact he seemed to revel in the attention. At least, every time Cindy chanced to see him with one of those eager pursuers, he would be flashing that crooked smile and being oh-so-charming as he escorted her to the door or left with her for lunch or dinner—or wherever the hell they were going!

Not that Cindy cared. It was certainly none of her business. But she was more than ever determined not to become one of the clan.

Still, it was hard to be in such close contact and remain immune. He was always dropping by her office, and each time she looked up to see his handsome face, so eager and alive, or heard his voice, husky with excitement, she had to struggle to maintain her strictly-business armor.

Trying to avoid Clay as much as she could, she made an effort to direct all conferences through Tom Morrison, his right-hand man. Morrison's office was across from hers, separated only by the office of Ann Eagle, the secretary she and Tom shared.

However, Morrison always deferred to Clay. And since Kencade had to make the final decision, important conferences always involved the three of them and would often take place over lunch in the executive dining room. As the discussions became heated, all her erotic sensations and fanciful thoughts quickly dispersed.

Cindy had had a very clear knowledge of the Kencade operation before she was employed there, and she'd come in equipped and eager to right what she thought was wrong. Her orderly accountant's attitude (check your capital and look before you leap) clashed with Kencade's aggressiveness (Hey, this is an opportunity—go for it!). Within two weeks the business discussions had become verbal battles. Sometimes she could convince him and Kencade would back down; sometimes she couldn't. But whatever the outcome and however fiery the encounter, his mood immediately switched when it was over and he would return to his calm good-natured disposition.

Cindy couldn't do this. She'd come to Kencade Enterprises determined to see that it achieved a solid financial base. And she was disconcerted to find that she had to fight as hard to keep finances in balance as she did to keep her emotions under control.

Tom Morrison, an older man, was as conservative in financial matters as Cindy, and she marveled that he managed to remain unperturbed by the risks Clay insisted on taking.

"I know he goes off half-cocked sometimes," Morrison said. "But he usually lands on his feet."

"So far," Cindy added, reluctant to admit that this was true. "There's always a first time to overextend."

Clay was scheduled to leave for London in a few days, and Cindy felt a surge of relief when she heard about his trip. She remembered Jane's warnings. Well, talking about job problems wasn't exactly an aphrodisiac but it *was* "heavy," and she needed a breather.

It was after one of their business blowups that Clay phoned to offer her a ride home. He'd promised Johnny he would come out to practice batting.

That was another problem, she thought, as she unconsciously chewed her thumbnail. The children weren't as close to Clay as they'd been to Dan. But they were getting there. Whenever the Jaguar stopped in the driveway, Jamey would call, "Here's Clay" and little Teri would run out to meet him. Later she would hear Clay instructing

Johnny. "Just relax. Keep your eye on the ball." And twice more she'd invited him to stay for dinner. Once he'd taken them all out and hadn't been at all bothered by Teri's mess or Jamey's chatter. He made things *fun*. He enjoyed the children. And he was comfortable to be with.

But she'd had a similar experience with Dan. And she knew about Kencade's reputation and how easily he could tire of a relationship.

Oh, yes, admit it, Cindy. You're beginning to like his company too much. And if she, an adult trying to guard herself against involvement with this very man, was being drawn in, what about the children, so unguarded and vulnerable? There ought to be some way to taper off the relationship.

"I think you should be careful about spoiling Johnny," she ventured as they drove out that day.

"Spoiling him? How?"

"I know you don't mean to. And it's really wonderful of you to help him. His batting has improved tremendously. But..." She fiddled with a button on her blouse. "Oh, you know children. You give them a little of your time and they expect all of it. I know how busy you are. You're getting ready to go to London and everything." She felt a little foolish. "Well, all I'm saying is, it won't be your fault, but Johnny might not understand when you don't have the time to give him."

He glanced at her sharply before turning his attention back to the bumper-to-bumper traffic. "You've changed your tactics, haven't you?"

"What do you mean?"

"Well, you're always advising me to take time to check things out, read the fine print, before signing a long-term contract." His tone was teasing and implied something that had nothing to do with Johnny. She gave the button such a twist that it popped off.

"That's different and you know it!" she blurted. "A relationship is not a business deal."

"Exactly. So why do you insist on keeping our relationship strictly business? Just what have you got against . . . getting to know me." He sang the words to the music of a well-known Rodgers and Hammerstein song, and she blushed as she saw the crooked smile twist his lips.

"Don't be ridiculous. It's not you," she lied. "It's just that I'm busy. You know that."

"I know you have a housekeeper who lives in during the week. So there's no reason you couldn't spend an evening with me. We could go to a play, have dinner out or anything you want. Why do you always turn me down?"

"Because I have to be at home. There are things I have to do. Help Johnny with his math. Take Jamey for swimming lessons and Teri to dancing. Anyway, I wasn't talking about me. I was talking about the children."

"Okay. The children." He frowned as he maneuvered the car into another lane. "You object to my coaching Johnny?"

"It's not that. It's just—"

"That you want me to promise I'll be there for him forever and ever, Amen."

"Of course I don't expect that!"

"Well, good, 'cause life's not like that. Today I'll pitch a few balls to Johnny and tomorrow I might be in Timbucktu. Or dead, like his dad."

"Or you might just walk away!" she said bitterly. He sounded so callous!

"Right. Some deals don't work out." He gave her another sharp glance. "I might just walk away. But Johnny's game might be a little better because we practiced

today. And he'll remember the fun. I hope so, anyway."
She watched his face harden as he drove toward the parkway exit. "You can't shelter those children from life, Cindy. People move on. Things change. Johnny's got to learn to enjoy the moment. So do you, Cindy. Time flies, and you might miss all the fun."

Enjoy the moment. There. He'd said it aloud. That was the kind of person he was. He could move in, have fun, move out.

Well, he can afford to be like that. I can't. I know I can't always shelter the children from life's sorrows and problems. But I'll protect them as much as I can.

She said no more on the subject. He wouldn't understand.

She was glad when he left for London.

During the ten days he was gone, she did her level best to protect his business interests. That was her job.

Not that he appreciated the protection. He hadn't been back two hours before he stormed into her office in a towering rage, demanding to know what the hell she meant by causing a foul-up on the Lantine Paint deal. Cynthia listened to his tirade until she could stand it no longer. Then she slammed a memo pad down on her polished oak desk and sprang from the coral cushions of her soft leather chair to glare into Clay Kencade's furious dark eyes.

"I was under the impression," she said through clenched teeth, "that you were paying for my advice."

"Right. For advice. Not your damned interfering instructions."

"I gave no instructions."

"How about 'hold off on bids for Lantine Paints'?"

" 'Until I have contacted Mr. Kencade and he—' "

"At which time the deal has been snatched. Signed, sealed and delivered to Carter, Incorporated."

"Send a thank-you note. They did you a favor."

"That's your opinion," he shouted.

"An opinion supported by fact." She sank back into her chair, trying to keep her temper under control. She spoke slowly and deliberately. "More than half the stores in the Lantine chain have been operating in the red for the past three years. Inventories are depleted and the only goodwill you'd get is a list of unpaid creditors and a host of dissatisfied customers."

"Which is exactly why I could have picked it up for a song. What the hell do I care about inventory and goodwill? I planned to bring them under the Forest label and operate—"

"For the next two years on a negative cash flow. Just as forty percent of your Forest stores are doing now."

"Damn it, Cindy. It takes time to revamp and revitalize."

"Exactly. Time and money. And that's why you should hold off on buying and give yourself time to catch up. Assuming you want to stay afloat. Here, let me show you...." She picked up a pencil and pulled a pad toward her. "Figures don't lie. The percentages are—"

"The hell with percentages!" He reached over and took the pencil from her. "I don't intend to get bogged down by your damn figures." He held the pencil, almost—but not quite—pointing it at her. She felt the tension between them vibrate like a taut string. "I want to explain something to you. Very simply. When opportunity knocks—I grab! And I'd advise you not to let an opportunity like Lantine Paint slip through my fingers again. Understood?"

"That sounds like a threat, Mr. Kencade." Anger seemed to form a knot in her stomach.

"No. No threat." The fury in his face was replaced by surprise. He seemed a little subdued as he tossed the pencil back onto the desk and shoved his hands in his pockets. "I was just trying to tell you something about the way I operate."

"Oh? Well, let me tell you something about the way I operate." She stood up again and spoke as if she couldn't get the words out fast enough. "When someone hires me to do a job, I do it to the best of my ability. As your acquisition accountant, I feel it's my duty to keep your credit line intact and see that your cash flow is never exceeded by acquisition and expansion."

"Afraid of taking risks?" The husky sensuous quality of his voice and a suggestive twinkle in his eyes made her start. She turned away, confused, wishing she could keep up with his changing moods.

"My job is to help you retain control of your finances," she said, her voice a little tremulous. "And if you don't want me to do that, say so and I'll resign now!"

"You can't resign. You're under contract." His low chuckle irritated her. She just couldn't get accustomed to these rapid, off-key changes. Like now—from raw anger to . . . to something she couldn't define.

"That's no problem," she retorted, fighting to keep the discussion on business. "If you go on the way you have been, you'll be so deep into bankruptcy, you'll be glad to release me!"

"Oh, no, my sweet. That will take more than bankruptcy." His wink was as intimate as a kiss, and she felt the heat stain her cheeks.

She was speechless as he walked out and shut the door.

CHAPTER SEVEN

CLAY KENCADE DRUMMED his fingers on his desk and stared into space.

"Something bugging you, Mr. K.?" Maggie asked as she gathered up the correspondence they had just gone over.

"Cynthia Rogers."

"Cindy?" Maggie leaned back in her chair. "But I thought she was working out quite well. She's very nice. And really engrossed in her work."

"Too damn engrossed! She's right on my tail every time I start to make a move. If she hasn't got everything tied up in a tight little financial knot, she thinks I'm making a mistake." He picked up a pencil, threw it down again. "How the hell does she think I got where I am? I was making deals when she was still playing with dolls."

"Oh, I'm sorry she's not working out. I thought—"

"Now wait a minute! I didn't say she wasn't working out. She's sharp. Never misses a detail when it comes to facts and figures. Even made me pull back on a couple of things. Maybe I need a little of that. And I can handle her. I let her check out the trees and I make up my own mind about buying the forest. I'm still the boss."

"Right." Maggie sat holding the folder and looking at him, obviously a bit puzzled. "So what's the problem? If you've worked out a good business relationship—"

"Well, I wasn't exactly thinking of business."

"Oh." She inclined her head. "But, I thought . . . Haven't you been out to Greenwich several times?"

"To see the boy."

"Boy? Oh, yes, she did tell me she has custody of her sister's three children. And she's so young. She must have her hands full."

"Yes, and stays scared to make a move for fear it'll be the wrong one. Same way she is in business, come to think of it," he mused.

"Oh, I see. So you go out there to see the boy." Maggie made a face. "Trying to get to her through the children?"

"No!" He frowned. "Hell, I didn't even know she had the children till I went out to her house. And then the kid— the oldest one—Johnny. He's nine. Just at the age when you stop playing baby games and go into what you think is real competition. Well, I guess it is, anyway. And the boy's starved for—well, a male model." Clay tilted back in his chair, his hands behind his head. "You know, Maggie, I was pretty lucky, having Pop. My first season in Little League I was so scared, positive I'd really blow it and mess up the team. Pop was great. I can hear him now. 'Cool it, kid. They're all rookies, just like you.' And he'd take me out behind the store and pitch a few balls." He sat up, swallowed hard. "Oh, hell, Maggie, I don't like to talk about Pop."

"I know. You two were so close."

"Well, he was always there for me." Clay sighed. "And the day I was at Johnny's game and he struck out twice, he threw down his bat and ran off crying. I understood just how he felt. Before I knew it, I'd promised to come out to his place and pitch a few balls to him. Now, whenever I go out there, he always wants to know when I'm coming back. Like he's afraid I won't."

"Got into something you can't get out of, huh?"

"Oh, no, I don't mind. Fact is, I rather enjoy it. He's a great kid—eager and works really hard. And you know something? He's getting good. I think he's going to be a great little ball player." He got up, walked to the window, stretched and turned to look at her. "I really like him. We have a lot of fun."

"I see." Maggie, who had not moved from her chair, looked at him. "And you like his aunt, too?"

"Cindy? I...yeah, I guess so." He ran his fingers through his hair, feeling a little puzzled. Why did he find her so appealing? All these weeks and still he hardly knew her. She was so careful to shut herself off. "It's like I only get a glimpse of the real Cindy every now and then," he said, as if explaining to himself as well as to Maggie. "Once, the night we had dinner in my apartment, that's the only time I've seen her relax. Just be herself, with nothing else on her mind, no agenda. Not that we talked about anything much. Just that she seemed carefree and warm and..." He stopped. That was the woman he wanted to see more of. The woman who had responded to his light...yes, almost casual kiss, with such fervor. As if in one unguarded moment she'd released her warm, sensuous inner self. He sighed. "I feel a little sorry for her, Maggie."

"Sorry?"

"Yeah. Because she never seems to have time to be herself. She's so busy looking after other people. She's a giver, Maggie. She's so busy trying to do everything and be everything for those kids that they don't have time to do or think for themselves. She's always protecting them." He chuckled. "Protecting me, too. She's spunky, I'll give her that. You ought to hear her fighting with me, trying to keep me from taking any risks that she thinks threaten my empire. Hell, I built the business on risks! But she means well. Like I said, she's a giver."

"You're a bit of a giver, yourself, Mr. K."

"Huh?"

"Tell me something. Why have you never married?"

The question coming out of the blue startled him. "Well, I don't know. Never thought of it. I guess I had my hands too full. You know how I had to hustle after Dad went bankrupt. And then, when he was sick for so long, I didn't have time for much else. Truth is, I don't know why I never married. Guess I've been too busy."

Maggie sniffed and stood up. "Not too busy to spend time with quite a few women."

He laughed, but he thought about that. There *had* been many women—good friends whom he liked. But not one with whom he wanted to spend his life. "Okay," he amended. "Maybe I've been too busy to form a close relationship."

"Or maybe it's just that you haven't met the right lady."

He shrugged. "Could be."

Maggie started to leave, but when she reached the door she turned back. "You know, Mr. K., you've had so many women chasing you, you've never had to chase them."

"Oh?"

"So you've never learned how."

"Come on, Maggie. What are you driving at?"

"Technique." She grinned. "I have an idea. These...er...business discussions you're always having with Ms Rogers."

"Go on," he said, giving her a skeptical look.

"Well, why couldn't they be extended to a dinner conference at...let's see...at the Tropicana where there's dancing. And where she might be persuaded to...just be herself. You wouldn't have to argue all evening, would you?"

"Do you suppose I haven't thought of that and suggested—"

"Don't suggest. Insist. After all, you're the boss." Maggie's eyes twinkled as she went out and shut the door.

THE INTERCOM BUZZED and Cindy heard her secretary say, "Mr. Kencade on the phone, Ms Rogers."

That was odd. He usually just barged into her office. In person.

"Yes, Clay," she said into the phone. They'd been on a first-name basis for some time now. Impossible to be formal in the midst of a heated business discussion. Or, she admitted, smiling to herself, in the midst of the children and baseball and peanut butter sandwiches.

"Cindy, I'm leaving for Denver tomorrow afternoon." To look at that decrepit tool plant, she guessed, as he went on to explain that was exactly what he intended to do.

"Listen," she said. "Before you do anything I want you to—"

"I know. That's why I'm calling. I know you've reviewed the financial data and I'd like to talk it over with you." Yes, he certainly ought to do that, she thought. "The thing is," he went on, "I'll be pretty busy today and my calendar is full in the morning. So I think perhaps we'd better do it this evening. Discuss it, I mean."

"Oh?"

"Let's see, my last meeting today will be near...oh, yes, the Tropicana. Could you meet me there around six? I'll have Maggie make a dinner reservation."

"I don't think I—"

"I wouldn't insist but I just don't see any other time."

"Well..."

"Thanks, Cindy, I'll see you tonight." He hung up and she slowly returned her phone to its cradle.

The Tropicana? Not exactly the place for a business conference. Cindy used to go there often, enjoying the quiet subdued atmosphere and the dancing... with Dan. Tonight with Clay... The tremor was involuntary and alive with a sweet tingling expectancy.

She wrenched her thoughts from the man, took her thumbnail out of her mouth and forced herself to think about business. The Denver plant. She took the report from her file and spread it on her desk. They really needed to talk about this before he went off the deep end.

Cindy had begun to get an inkling of the way Clay operated and realized that he usually had a good plan. She was glad she'd kept him from picking up the Lantine chain, but she had to admit that the Forest Paint Stores were really coming along. Clay had made a man named Hank Elkins executive manager and had given him twelve percent of the stock. Hank was knocking himself out to streamline the operation, and earnings were increasing. He was accomplishing this by giving the unit managers the same incentives Clay had given him—decision-making powers, performance bonuses and stock ownership.

Cindy tapped her pencil against the report as she thought about that. Hodgepodge as Clay's enterprises appeared, they shared one striking characteristic. The management of each Kencade-owned company and the members of their boards of directors always held significant chunks of stock, which gave them a strong voice in running the show as well as a stake in the outcome. "It's only good business," Clay had said. He was right.

She looked down at the report. Denver Tools. Not a consistent commodity, like paint. As she saw it, the slump in profits had come not from bad management, but from an outmoded product. The company made tools for machinery that was rapidly being replaced by newer, more modern models. So why should Clay even go to look at the plant? Yes, they needed to talk.

She picked up the phone and called to cancel Jamey's swimming lesson. Then she phoned Mrs. Stewart to tell her she would be out late, asking her to please check Johnny's homework.

THE TROPICANA WAS just as she remembered it, with the hanging plants and foliage cleverly placed to give it the appearance of a tropical paradise. With tables tucked away in obscure little booths, it was a retreat for lovers.

"Good evening, Mr. Kencade," said the hostess. "Your table is ready."

"Thank you," he said and took Cindy's hand. They followed the hostess to one of the obscure booths. She seated them and gave Kencade a warm smile before she hurried away.

Cindy couldn't help asking, "Do you come here often?" If so, why had she never seen him? But maybe, she thought, she hadn't been looking at anyone but Dan then.

"Not too often. Just sometimes when I leave a board meeting that's held in the vicinity."

Cindy looked across at his handsome chiseled features and compelling dark eyes. Yes, she thought, any woman who'd seen him would remember. She swallowed and composed herself.

"I've been looking over the data concerning the tool company," she said. "And I think—"

"How about a cocktail?"

She nodded, feeling a little nervous.

"Margaritas, I think," he said to the waitress. "That's a nice before-dinner drink, don't you agree?" he asked

Cindy. She nodded and was about to bring up the tool company report again, but he held a finger to his lips. "Sssh. I like this song."

The combo, located some distance from them, was partially concealed by foliage and blurred by the soft lights. A woman wearing a slinky lamé dress sang in a husky voice about the pangs and passions of awakening love. For a moment, Cindy was captivated by the haunting strains of music and the words of the song. She tried to remain unaware of Clay's steady gaze and felt relieved when the song ended and the waitress brought their drinks. She sipped hers, liking the salty taste.

"This is very refreshing." She smiled at him. "You always seem to choose the right drink."

"Thank you."

"Well, now," she said, pulling a notepad from her purse.

"Give me a break, Cindy. I've just come from a hectic board meeting. Let me finish my drink before you make me talk business. Give me a chance to relax."

"That's a laugh," she said rather crisply. "Except when you get into one of your rages, I've never seen you when you weren't relaxed."

"And I've never seen you when you were." He leaned toward her. "What makes Cindy Rogers happy and relaxed?"

"Look, we'd better made good use of this time. I canceled Jamey's swimming lesson so we could—"

"Swimming. Do you swim, Cindy?"

"Look, I swim. I play tennis." *Lord, when have I had time to do either?* "I do lots of things and I'm always very relaxed. Now, I brought these figures so—"

"Speaking of figures, do you know how lovely yours is, Cindy?"

"What?"

"Not a model's figure, exactly. You're not tall enough," he said as if he were assessing her. "I think it's the way you carry yourself. So erect and graceful. And when you walk, swinging along... Have you ever noticed how people watch you walk?"

"No. I... Don't be silly." She took a gulp of her drink. "People don't watch me."

"I do. Sometimes I linger in the lobby just to see you hurry by. I like the way you walk, Cindy."

"Oh." He was flirting with her and she decided to ignore it. She bent to her notebook. "About this Denver venture. I don't think you're really aware of what's going on."

"I don't think you're aware, either."

She stared at him. "What do you mean?"

"I don't believe you're aware of that music."

She swallowed. She was very aware of the music. As aware as she was of the way he was looking at her, as aware as she was of the desperate pounding of her heart. "Oh," she burst out. "This is a terrible place to do business!"

"I couldn't agree more. So—let's not try." He smiled and extended his hand. "Shall we dance?"

It was wonderful. Being held by him, absorbing his nearness, his chin against her temple, his hand gently caressing her back. It was wonderful to be dancing again, moving in rhythm to the lilting music, in rhythm to each other. Wonderful. This moment with this man. Cindy spent the rest of the evening in a euphoric haze, hardly aware of what she ate or drank or what was said. She was aware only of an exhilarating enchantment. A feeling, sweet and sensual, that pulsated between them and drew them closer. When they drove back to Greenwich, her head was on his shoulder.

At the station she picked up her car and he followed her home. This time she did invite him in for "a cup of coffee before you have to drive back to the city."

In the quiet living room, she switched on a soft lamp and started to move toward the kitchen.

"Not yet," he said, and pulled her into his arms. His kiss was gentle, tentative, but awakened such a fiery desire within her that she pressed closer, opening her lips to his and winding her arms around him. In immediate response, his mouth took complete possession of hers, the kiss slowly deepening.

She melted into his embrace with reckless abandon, her fingers caressing his face and tangling in his hair.

"Oh, Cindy." It was a hoarse whisper, as if his emotions were as shattered, as uncontrollable, as hers. He placed small, intimate kisses on her eyelids, her temple and her lips. When he buried his mouth in the hollow of her throat, she felt drugged with desire. A lethargic yielding seemed to overwhelm her and she turned her face into his shoulder, trying to resist, trying to draw away.

As if he understood, his hand slipped from her waist slowly and reluctantly. "Time for coffee?" he asked, smiling at her with gentle indulgence.

He followed her into the kitchen and watched while she made the coffee. She didn't feel awkward this time. She felt comfortable, relaxed. She smiled at him and talked of inconsequential things until the coffee was ready. Then she filled two mugs and pushed one across the breakfast bar to him.

"Come and sit with me on the sofa," he said, as he started to get off the bar stool.

"No. Stay right where you are. We have to talk business now."

He sat back down, but frowned at her. "Oh, Cindy, don't get started on that tool company again."

"But isn't that what this evening was all about?"

"Not exactly."

His teasing grin made her blush. The tremors began once more as she remembered the sweet sensation of being in his arms. His eyes seemed to hold the memory too, and she looked away.

"Now," she said, trying to collect her thoughts. "You wanted to discuss this proposed deal with the tool company."

"So I did." He took a sip of coffee. "Good coffee, Cindy. Okay, about the company. I looked over the reports you gave me last week and I've already made up my mind."

"To buy?" Had he really discounted everything she'd said, all her warnings and suggestions?

"Yes. I've started negotiations. You see, what I plan—"

"Wait a minute. You've already made up your mind? Just tell me one thing. What was tonight's meeting all about?"

His mouth twisted in that grin. "You enjoyed it, didn't you?"

"That's not the point!" she snapped, her face burning at the thought of how thoroughly she *had* enjoyed the evening. "The fact is that you didn't want to talk about the Denver plant at all. You don't care about my opinion!" She'd spent so much time going over the figures, analyzed things so carefully.

"Listen, Cindy, you don't understand. I only wanted—"

"Oh, yes, I understand. And I resent it. If you don't care what I think, if you have no regard for my professional opinion, why did you hire me?"

"Now, wait a minute. I have a great deal of regard for your opinion. I always study your reports."

"And then you do exactly what you please!"

"I think I do have that prerogative." He sounded puzzled and just a little annoyed.

"Granted. You are the boss. But let's get this one thing straight. Being the boss doesn't give you the right to manipulate me."

"What do you mean by that?"

"I mean this is the second time you've tricked me."

"Tricked you?"

"By scheduling a meeting to discuss one thing when you have something else on your mind." Ugly thoughts pricked at her like sharp, little needles. Jane's warning. "Office affairs." All those women...

"Something else?" he prompted, his gaze level.

"Well, you certainly didn't have business on your mind. And I'm not one of your easy—" She broke off, more furious at herself than at him. She had fallen into his arms, submitted to his embraces as hungrily as any of those eager women who haunted his office. She swallowed. "I don't appreciate being forced into a situation that—"

"Forced?"

"Coerced then!" How dare he sit there looking so smug and innocent! Interrogating her as if he didn't know exactly what she meant. If he hadn't said it was business she would never have... "You can't deny that you used your position as my employer to...to coerce me into an evening of...of..."

"Yes?" He was standing now, and there was a glint, almost hostile, in his eyes.

She stood up to face him. "Let's put it this way. I'm an accountant. A darn good one! Sex is not part of my profession!"

His face when livid. "You don't mean... You're not trying to accuse me— You are! You're implying sexual harassment!"

"No! I didn't say that."

"You might not have said it. But I got the message. Well, I won't be harassing you any further. Good night."

She stood with her hand pressed over her mouth until she heard the front door slam behind him. Then, suddenly, she no longer felt angry.

She felt devastated.

CHAPTER EIGHT

CLAY RAN TWICE his usual distance around the park. Fast.

It didn't help. He was still furious when he got out of the shower, and viciously slapped shaving cream on his face.

The hell with Cynthia Rogers! Who the devil did she think she was! More to the point, what kind of guy did she think he was?

Being the boss doesn't give you the right to manipulate me. And that tight defiant look on her face! As if he— A sharp nick on his chin made him wince. He put down the razor and dabbed at the cut with a tissue, picked up the razor and started again.

Never had he tried to manipulate a woman into his arms! He'd never had to.

You manipulated her.

No. Not into his arms. The razor moved slowly across his face as he thought about it. Yes, he'd set up the whole thing as business. But he'd done it for her. To get her out— away from the kids and away from work. She was always so tense and serious about everything. Forever biting her nails and worrying about doing everything right. He'd wanted her to get out and just enjoy being herself.

She had enjoyed it. They'd danced, her slender willowy body moving as gracefully as when she walked. But not so purposefully. She danced freely, recklessly, abandoning herself to the music and the gaiety of the evening. He had liked watching her. Her face alive with the joy of the moment, the hazel eyes twinkling up at him as if . . . well, as if she liked being with him.

And, yes, the evening had been special for him, too. Once again he'd caught a glimpse of the woman she kept hidden behind all that intensity. The woman who appealed to him so strongly. He remembered how she'd leaned comfortably against him on the drive back, her tousled hair soft and light beneath his chin and that faint fresh odor of baby powder tickling his senses. It had felt so right. Later, standing close to her in the semidarkness of the living room, he hadn't been able to resist her temptingly curved lips. She had come willingly into his arms and returned his kiss with such a provocative yielding that passion flooded through him like a warm rain. He'd been filled with a desire he had never felt for any other woman. It had taken real effort to release her, for he'd sensed that her hunger matched his own.

But he'd been wrong. So that was that.

He sure wasn't going to be like Pop, who had never accepted the fact that the only woman he ever loved didn't love him.

Love? What made him think about love?

He splashed after-shave on his face, cursing as he felt the cut sting, then he flung aside the towel and went in to dress.

He had an unusually busy day at the office. Constant phone calls, a steady round of people being ushered in and out, details to go over with Maggie and Tom before he left for Denver. About eleven there was a bit of a lull. He leaned back in his chair, closed his eyes and wondered why he felt so lonely.

Maggie buzzed. "Mrs. Daniels is on the line. Will you take it, Mr. K.?"

"Sure. Why not?" Poor Lisa. She tried to play the happy, liberated divorcée. But she was still grieving over her ex. "Hi, Lisa," he said into the phone.

"Well, hello, stranger," came her familiar sultry voice. "Where have you been keeping yourself?"

"Well, I—"

"Never mind. I forgive you. Now listen, I have the most fabulous plan for tonight." She was lonely, too, he thought, and was almost sorry he had to turn her down.

"Not tonight, Lisa. I'm leaving for Denver this afternoon."

"On business?" she asked.

"Strictly business," he assured her.

"Well, in that case, why don't I come along with you?"

When he laughingly demurred, saying she wouldn't enjoy it very much, she protested that she certainly would. And that she might even be of some help to him if Kencade Enterprises was extending into Denver; she had a cousin there who wielded a great deal of influence. "Anyway," she cajoled, "wouldn't you just love to have a delightful companion along on a tiresome old business trip?"

"Sure," he said, thinking, *Why the hell not!*

She said she'd check with Maggie about the flight, and hung up.

Later Maggie came in with a little insinuating smile on her face, and informed him that Mrs. Daniels had managed to get a reservation on the same flight that afternoon.

"Okay," he said.

"And," Maggie continued, "she'll be here in the office at three-thirty to catch a ride on the helicopter to the airport."

"Okay," he said again. But something about the expression on Maggie's face made him add, "She has a cousin in Denver. Chamber of commerce, Rotary Club—all that stuff. Might be a good connection."

"Uh-huh."

"What do you mean, 'uh-huh'?"

"I've never known you to worry about connections before." Maggie gave a little shrug. "But then, Mrs. Daniels is so thoughtful about these little details. She's so... efficient. I suppose that's the right word."

"Oh, wipe that silly grin off your face and bring me Ascot's file, will you?" Lisa was good company. And if she wanted to tag along, well... why the hell not?

CINDY SPENT a restless night, reviewing over and over in her mind the events of the evening and the altercation with Clay. The next morning as she entered the station and found a seat on the crowded train, she was still haunted by the look on Clay's face. She could tell he was shocked and deeply hurt by her accusation.

And truly, she hadn't meant it the way he'd taken it.

Sexual harassment? He hadn't asked for anything she hadn't willingly given. Oh, she was well aware that there were men who took advantage of their positions. She also knew Clay wasn't one of them. She groaned in embarrassment. Why had she overreacted like this? Anyway, she'd always believed she could gracefully reject any advance that didn't appeal to her. Even if it came from her boss.

Ah, that's it, isn't it, Cindy? With great good sense and foresight, she'd planned to reject any advance made by Clay Kencade. *And what burns you up is that you didn't— couldn't—reject him. Face it. Just to look at him sets you on fire.* And when he'd touched her, there was only feeling. She recalled the hot waves of pleasure that swirled inside her and the way she'd been consumed by an unfamiliar need, a need that clamored to be fulfilled.

Cindy rested her burning head against the cool window of the coach, remembering that it was he who had pulled away. At the time she'd been grateful for his gentle understanding. She had felt so comfortable with him. So happy. She'd made the coffee, still glowing from the warmth of his touch, and then—

She sat up, the surge of anger returning. He'd manipulated her. He hadn't planned to talk about business at all. And if she hadn't believed it was a business meeting she would never have gone out with him. She had sensed from the first how vulnerable she was, so she'd determined to keep their relationship on a strictly business level.

She was a darn good accountant! Just what Mr. Lucky-Know-It-All Clay Kencade needed—if he didn't want to get unlucky in a hurry. His cash flow was dwindling, his credit was stretched to the limit, and he needed that broken tool factory like he needed a hole in the head. And that was what she'd planned to tell him last evening before he got her so muddled that she—

The elderly woman sitting next to her touched her hand. "Are you all right, dear? You look so ill."

Cindy swallowed and tried to smile. "It's...er...it's just that I have something on my mind. You know how it is."

"Indeed I do, dearie. I'm glad you're all right. And don't let it worry you so, whatever it is. Oh, here we are. Time to get off."

Cindy tried to compose her thoughts as she joined the line of passengers leaving the train. She tried to assess the facts with her usual scrupulous honesty.

Number one. She owed Clay an apology. He was a single man, free to make any advances he chose. If she was stupid enough to fall immediately into his arms, that was her problem.

Number two. Clay Kencade owed her an apology. She was doing a bang-up job for him. If he absolutely discounted her opinions, ignored the facts she so carefully gathered, then he was insulting her, belittling her professional skills.

Number three. She could think of only one way to solve both problems. Resign.

She planned to hand him her official notice in person. Today. At this point she felt he'd offer no objection, contract or not. She wanted to clear out before he returned. When she arrived at the office she told Maggie to let her know as soon as he had a few minutes free—it was imperative that she see him before he left for Denver.

At around three o'clock, Maggie finally called her. "This is his first free time, Cindy. And you'll have to hurry. He's leaving in half an hour."

He was sitting at his desk, but stood up when she came into his office. Always a gentleman, she thought with some irony.

"You wanted to see me, Ms Rogers?" he asked, his face cold and unsmiling.

This was not going to be easy.

"Last night . . ." She swallowed and looked up at him. "I think you misunderstood. I didn't mean to imply that . . . what you thought."

"That's a relief. I think," he added with just a trace of sarcasm in his voice.

"It's just that we went out to discuss a specific work-related problem. Or so I thought. And then, well, things got a little out of hand. Possibly it was the atmosphere. The . . . chemistry." She paused, not wanting to offend him again. It had been her fault as much as his. "It's just that sometimes people give off signals they don't intend to. And, well, we never got around to discussing what I thought . . . what we intended to discuss."

"Look, Cindy, I get the message. You're saying let's stick to business, right? I get it. Okay."

"Yes. But something else, too. We're on a different wavelength, even in business."

"What do you mean?"

"I mean you're wasting money. Paying me for advice you don't intend to take. Like this tool company."

"That's not true, Cindy. I read your report very carefully."

"And decided to buy the company anyway."

"Because this is the time. Look . . ." He ran a hand through his hair in distraction. "I'm used to working alone and sometimes I barge right in without taking the time to explain all the reasons for my decision. I know exactly what you said—profits down, outmoded product. But you see," he went on, "I plan to change the product."

"Your cash flow won't—" Making changes would require even more of an outlay.

"I know. I know." He quoted figures verbatim that she thought he hadn't even read. "You see I do pay attention. I may have to sell something else to swing this. But—" He glanced at his watch. "I plan to talk that over with you when I return. I may be able to do something on the other end to lower the price. Stock and management options, that kind of thing. Stevens, the president, is in a bind. But basically he's good at what he does and . . ." He went on talking and all at once she saw it. This was Clay Kencade, man of business. All business. She saw the excitement in his eyes, heard it in his voice. A new venture. Moving fast.

Too fast?

As if he read the question in her eyes, he laughed. "I guess we *will* have to dump something."

"We will if you're going on with this."

"Well, look things over, would you? And decide what we ought to consider selling." He checked his watch again. "No time now. We'll talk it over when I get back."

"Yes," she agreed. She forgot that she'd intended to resign. He did listen. He did need her.

"And Cindy..." He looked down at her seriously and she thought she saw a flicker of sadness in his eyes. "I understand and I promise. Business only. Okay?" He held out his hand.

"All right," she said and took his hand. "Have a good trip, Clay."

"And be ready to catch hell when I get back?" he asked, chuckling warmly.

"At least be ready to make some changes," she answered, laughing as he opened the door for her.

A stunningly beautiful woman in a smart beige dress stood talking to Maggie. She turned when the door opened, and flinging back a mass of honey-blond hair, rushed past Cindy to Clay.

"You'd better come on. We've got to hurry."

Cindy gave a polite nod and walked quickly past. But she caught the whiff of expensive perfume and heard the woman say, "I sent my bags up to the helicopter, but I really didn't know what to bring. You didn't say how long we'd be staying."

Although Cindy went into her own office and shut the door—hard—the sultry voice still echoed in her ears. That woman, that beautiful, stunning exquisite woman, was going to Denver with Clay. She was going to share the excitement. She would accompany him to his meetings, join him for lunch, have dinner with him in romantic, softly lit restaurants. She would be held in his arms.

Cindy was appalled by the quick stab of jealousy.

Because last night *she'd* been in his arms. Because she'd been caught up in a sweet intoxicating fervor. *Because you were being kissed by an expert, a man of vast experience!*

No one should know that better than she. Hadn't Jane read to her from all those tabloid and magazine articles? "Clay Kencade, man of many affairs, many women." And hadn't she seen with her own eyes the daily trek of hopefuls to his office? She vowed again never to be one of them.

Maybe last night was a good thing. She might have made a fool of herself but at least she'd got her point across. At least now there was an understanding between her and Clay. Strictly business.

Good.

She sat at her desk and fought hard to hold back the tears.

CLAY RETURNED from Denver Wednesday afternoon. It had been a productive trip, businesswise.

But a mistake to take Lisa. He'd had no time for her.

Come on, buddy. You didn't want to make the time.

Her cousin's car had met them at the airport to drive them to his ranch about an hour's drive from Denver for a weekend house party. Lisa had been furious with Clay because he wouldn't accompany her, pleading a scheduled golf game with Stevens the next morning.

"If you have time to play golf, you have time to come to a party," she had stormed. Women didn't understand how much business was covered on a golf course, he thought wryly.

He never made it to the ranch in spite of her many calls, and wasn't in when she returned to the hotel Monday evening. It was a complete surprise to him when she turned up in his room early Tuesday morning. "I called room service and ordered breakfast for both of us," she'd announced with a winsome smile.

He sensed that she had more than breakfast in mind and was glad that he had the excuse of Stevens already waiting downstairs for him.

Lisa had stamped her well-groomed foot and complained, "I don't know why you invited me on this trip, Clay. Honestly, you haven't spent one moment with me!"

"Let me remind you that you invited yourself. I told you it was business."

"Well, just go back to your business then. I'm going home!" She ran out, almost crashing into the waiter who was wheeling in the breakfast cart.

The cloud of her perfume mingled with the smell of fresh coffee as Clay watched her go.

Why did I let her come along in the first place? Clay wondered. But he knew why. Because at the time she asked he was feeling lonely, and because there was a time when things would have been different.

Now, all during this hectic week, whenever he had time to look up from the figures Stevens kept throwing at him, there was only one person on his mind.

This was crazy. He'd have to stop thinking about Cindy Rogers.

And he hadn't been quite fair with Lisa. He'd take her out to dinner and apologize. But he wouldn't allow her to con him into any more trips.

Now that he was back at his desk, his mind turned to business. Just as he'd expected, Stevens had gone along with all of his suggestions. Clay told Maggie to schedule a meeting with Cindy and Tom for the next morning so they could work out the details. So far, so good, he thought, just as Maggie buzzed.

"A Johnny Atwood on the line, Mr. K. Sounds like a child."

Oh, Cindy's boy. He picked up the phone. "Hi, Johnny. How are you?"

"Okay. I got a hit Saturday."

"All right! That's great!"

"Just a two-base hit. I got to second, but I stole third. And then Davey got a hit and I scored."

"Good for you. I wish I'd been there to see it. I was out of town."

"I know. Cindy told me. We won—18 to 7."

"Well, good for the Semco Cubs. See, I told you. Lots of practice is all it takes. Right on, champ!"

"Clay, are you busy?"

"Busy?"

"Well, Cindy said you might be. And you might not be coming—I mean, you wouldn't have time to be coming out here so much."

It was a plaintive cry and it pulled at Clay. "Hey, guy, I'm never too busy for you."

"You're not?"

"'Course not. How about Monday? Same time?"

"Okay!" There was such a ring of joy in Johnny's voice, Clay knew he wouldn't miss that appointment. And he didn't even know what Maggie had arranged for him. Whatever it was, he'd change it.

"Keep up the practice. See you on Monday," he said before he hung up. Then he leaned back in his chair.

Cindy. He'd been able to banish her from his mind most of the time he was away. But not always. At the oddest moments her impish little face would swim before him.

And since he'd walked into the office he'd been aching to get a glimpse of her.

He'd just have to get over that. She had set limits and he intended to respect them. But he sure didn't intend to let the boy down.

"JOHNNY TELEPHONED Clay at his office today," Jamey said.

Cindy, shuffling through the day's mail, hesitated. She never knew whether to scold Jamey for tattling or to reward him for passing on the valuable tidbits of information she would never otherwise receive. And Clay! Just as she'd feared—

"He wanted Clay to come out and pitch balls and he asked him and Clay said—"

Cindy held an envelope against Jamey's mouth. "Don't you think you'd better let Johnny talk about his own activities?"

"Yeah, Jamey! Shut up!" Johnny scolded at his brother, who retreated behind Cindy. "And I didn't ask him, Cindy. I didn't!"

"But Johnny, Mr. Kencade is a very busy man," she said gently. "You shouldn't disturb him at his office. Remember I explained that to you?" Goodness, what did Clay think!

"I'm sorry. I just wanted to tell him I got that hit and we won and all. And, Clay...he said he wasn't too busy." His little face looked so anxious and hopeful now that her heart turned over. "And he said he'd come out here Monday. That's all right, isn't it? If he wants to come?"

Cindy relented, feeling a wave of gratitude toward Clay. Just in from Denver, with loads of calls and appointments waiting, but he had responded to Johnny's unspoken plea. She remembered his words—*Tomorrow I might be in Timbuktu.... But Johnny's game might be a little better because we practiced today...*

She would let Johnny have his "todays."

CHAPTER NINE

THE THREE OF THEM, Clay, Tom and Cindy, had remained in the conference room for more than an hour, discussing the various projects, trying to decide which one was best to sell. But now Clay seemed to have made his decision. Cindy stared at him in consternation.

"Sell Scandinavian Shipping Lines!" She couldn't believe it. "But that's your biggest money-maker."

"So it ought to bring in plenty. That's what you want, isn't it? Cash?"

"I'm thinking more in terms of cash flow, Clay." She glanced at the papers scattered on the conference table, at all the data she'd collected on each project. She'd thoroughly analyzed them all. Her voice rose as she gestured toward the papers. "You have an imbalance here. Too many companies operating with a negative cash flow. Can't you see that?" She looked across the conference table, appealing to Tom.

Tom clenched his pipe between his teeth and shrugged.

"None of them will bring in as much as Scandinavian," Clay said.

"Oh, I don't know. Take this shopping center you plan." She tapped the paper with her finger. "If you opened it up for bids you might be surprised. This is prime property." Valuable for someone who was not already overextended, she thought. "Great potential, of course. But now it's nothing to you but a drain. Taxes, demolition and development. It'll be at least a year before this will even begin to pay off. If you put it up for sale—''

"No!" Clay's voice was sharp and decisive. He stood up. "We'll sell the shipping line. Get on it, Tom. And you have the notes on Denver Tools. Work it out, will you?" He glanced at his watch. "I've got an appointment with a packaging engineer now." Without another word he picked up his pen from the table, jammed it into his pocket and strode out.

Cindy turned her exasperation on Tom. "You ought to stop smoking. It's bad for your health."

"Yep. Too much a habit, though." He flashed a look at her. "And you needn't bite my head off because you're mad at Clay."

"Oh, I could just shake him," she said. "Why he wants to sell a perfectly good shipping line that's going smoothly and bringing in profits is beyond me!"

"That's it. Don't you see?"

"No, I don't," she muttered, getting up to collect her papers.

"Going smoothly. Which means no challenge."

"Oh, I do see!" She slammed folders together. "He prefers the challenge of an outdated plant already deep in the red!"

"You got it! Stevens, this guy who owns the biggest hunk of Denver Tools, is in a jam. Damned if I know which Clay likes more—taking on a tough challenge or getting somebody out of a jam." Tom pointed the stem of his pipe at Cindy. "His father was in a jam once."

"Oh?"

"Which reminds me, Cindy. Lay off that shopping center. That's the heart of Kencade Enterprises."

"Oh?" She looked down at him. "How so?"

"That's where it started. Didn't you know?"

She shook her head.

"Yep. Clay practically grew up in that five-story building on the southwest corner. It was his father's dry goods store. Harry Kencade. I managed the men's department and Maggie was Harry's secretary."

"Oh. You worked for Clay's father."

"Yep. When Clay was just a little tyke, always running in and out." He chuckled. "I remember one time he got lost. We hunted everywhere for two hours. We were all frantic."

"But you found him?" Cindy impatiently watched Tom relight his pipe. "Where?" she asked, the acrid smell of tobacco filling her nostrils as Tom drew on his pipe several times.

"Under a display table of men's sweaters. He'd been reading there and fell asleep. Always reading. Bright kid. Maggie used to call him Little Mr. K. Now she just leaves off the 'little.'" Tom laughed and Cindy imagined a small boy with Clay's winsome smile and a lock of dark hair falling across his forehead.

"So he spent a lot of time at the store?" She was eager to hear more, and as Tom seemed in a reminiscent mood, she sat down again to listen.

"Yep. Especially after Harry's wife left. It seemed like all Harry cared about was his business and his boy. It hit him hard when he lost the business."

"What happened?"

"I don't know really. I guess the neighborhood changed and Harry didn't change with it. Anyway, the business went into receivership and he had to close up the store. I moved on to another job. But Maggie—her husband was living then and she stayed around with no pay to help Harry clear out. So she was there the day he keeled over at his desk. Heart attack. She says she was scared out of her wits. But she called an ambulance and got hold of Clay. He was working part-time at his college bookstore." Again Tom pointed his pipe at Cindy. "Tell you one thing. I've had confidence in him since that day. He wasn't quite eighteen, but he took charge."

"Of course. He would," she said thoughtfully.

"Yep. And it was rough going, I'll tell you. Clay moved like a dynamo, running back and forth to school and the hospital and trying to save the building."

"The building?" Clay asked. "I thought he lost everything."

"Not the building, though it came close. Maggie thinks that triggered the heart attack—when Harry realized he was going to have to sell the building. But he didn't. Somehow Clay managed...." Tom looked down at his pipe, which had gone out again. "It seemed like he thought he should have been there helping his father instead of going to school. He was involved in sports and all—great basketball player." Tom paused to relight his pipe and take a few puffs. "But he gave all that up and took over the business."

Cindy watched the puffs of smoke and listened intently while Tom told her how Clay had somehow secured a loan and remodeled the building, dividing it into rental units for other businesses, including a coin laundry that Clay operated himself. She was presented with a different picture of "lucky" Clay Kencade, "thirty-six-year-old millionaire." Through Tom's eyes she saw a skinny, hardworking college kid who gave up sports and dating to care for his father and run a business.

"Clay had a manager's office with Harry's name on the door in big letters," Tom said. "But Harry could never work more than part-time. Clay hired me, supposedly as Harry's assistant, to really manage the place. Clay worked hard, but it all paid off. Five years later he'd picked up three more businesses and Kencade Enterprises was launched. He was on his way."

"These other businesses," Clay asked. "I suppose they were bankruptcies...or on the verge?"

Tom chuckled. "I don't pretend to know much about psychology," he said, as he emptied the contents of his pipe into an ashtray. "But it does seem that the fix his dad was in gave Clay a real feeling for losers. He hates to see a business close down and put people out of work."

Like Denver Tools, Cindy thought.

"And I guess there's something to this 'cast your bread upon the water' stuff." Tom took a pouch from his pocket and began to refill his pipe. "It seems like Clay never has money on his mind. But he's a millionaire just the same. I don't think you need to worry, Cindy. Like I say, he always lands on his feet."

She felt subdued and very thoughtful as this new image of Clay Kencade emerged, filling her mind and her heart. She wanted to ask more questions, hear more stories about Clay. But she knew that if she so much as mentioned his name her feelings would spill over and Tom would guess.

"I think it's okay for you to smoke, Tom," she said, standing up again and picking up her folders.

"Oh?"

"Sure. You never really smoke. All you do is wave that pipe around. When you're not relighting or refilling it, that is."

Tom's laugh followed her as she went out.

It was from Maggie that Cindy learned more. One day the two of them lunched together, and Cindy, feeling more composed now, said that Tom had told her something of Clay's early life. She hoped she sounded indifferent enough to fool the older woman.

"Oh?" Maggie's look was speculative.

"About—" Cindy toyed with her salad "—how he saved his father's business."

"He saved more than that," Maggie said without hesitation. "He saved Harry's life."

"Yes. Tom told me that Mr. Kencade was truly wrapped up in his business and Clay saved the building, started things over again."

"Oh, that." Maggie shrugged. "That was inevitable. Clay's a born entrepreneur. What I meant was the way he gave his father incentive—keeping up his interest, consulting him about every move. As if it was Harry and not Clay who made the decisions." Maggie paused to bite into her chicken sandwich. After a moment, she said, "But I meant more than that. He gave his father a reason to go on living and he also gave him the best of care. Special meals. Remodeling that old brownstone where they lived because his father wouldn't move. Air-conditioning, the elevator—anything to keep Harry comfortable."

Cindy remembered Clay's casual remarks. Put in central air-conditioning... Had to learn to cook because Pop couldn't. Never an indication that he had done it *for* his father.

"He must have really loved his father," she said, speaking her thoughts aloud.

"I guess that's the word," Maggie said. "Because he not only took care of him, he spent time with him. Going for walks together and to the golf course. Luring him back to the office. He kept Harry going for nine years, when the doctors had only given him two." She put down her coffee cup and looked earnestly at Cindy. "Clay was really busy, too, trying to make a go of the business. He didn't have much spare time and what he did have, he spent with his father. No time for dating or anything for himself."

"Well, he's sure making up for it now," Cindy said, a little tartly. The stream of women she saw going in and out of Clay's office couldn't all be there on business. Especially the ones who left with him.

"Naturally." Maggie rolled her eyes. "He's handsome, single and rich. Women come out of the woodwork after him. Can't blame 'em, though." She shook her head and laughed. "I'd be after him myself if I weren't old enough to be his mother. Clay Kencade is a really special guy."

Cindy was silent, realizing the truth of this. Realizing how much she'd learned about him in the past few days.

"But it burns me up!" Maggie said, pushing her plate away. "All these women. Most of them don't even *know* how special he is. They're only after his money. And Clay...well, he's such a...a man!"

"Yes," Cindy agreed, amused at the vehemence with which Maggie had uttered the word *man*.

"Men are such idiots, Cindy," Maggie continued. "They fall every time for that 'oh, you're so wonderful' mush, and never even realize what some women are really after. I'm so afraid the wrong woman will get hold of Clay." She leaned confidingly toward Cindy. "He needs someone special—just as special as he is. A woman soft enough to really understand and love him, but strong enough to tell him when he's wrong." She broke off to say "Yes, please" to the waiter, who had arrived with fresh coffee.

Cindy waited until the waiter had refilled their cups and moved away before she asked what she could not help asking. "Does he...I mean, is there someone...special that he's interested in?"

Maggie seemed to consider this. "It's hard to tell. I thought for a while he was interested in this schoolteacher that one of his stepsisters is pushing. She's a rather attractive little thing. But now, well, he seems to be focusing on this Lisa Daniels. He took her to Denver with him, you know,'' she added, casting Cindy a significant look.

"Oh, yes. I saw her.'' Cindy's heart gave a sickening thud as she recalled the lovely woman with the mass of golden-blond hair.

"Of course, I don't know if he's *really* interested in her. Maybe he's just treating her as one of his pet charities.''

"Pet charities. I didn't know he had any.''

"Oh, yes, a few. Like that home for troubled boys that was a lot of help to one of his stepbrothers. Clay's been its main support for some years.''

"I didn't know that. At least, I've seen no indication.'' She thought of taxes and was momentarily diverted from Clay's romantic interests.

Maggie shrugged.

"And this Lisa Daniels. She's in need of money?'' Cindy asked, thinking that she certainly didn't look it!

"Oh, no. She's got plenty of money of her own. She's a crybaby. She's been crying ever since her husband left her—mostly on Clay's shoulder. He's a real softie, you know. But lately...'' Maggie grinned. "Seems to me she's been doing more maneuvering than crying. I believe she's determined to make Clay a replacement for her last husband. And she just might do it! She's a very clever woman.''

Cindy suddenly threw down her napkin and said through tight lips, "I'd better go. Lots to do. See you later, Maggie.''

CHAPTER TEN

CINDY COULDN'T GET Maggie's words out of her mind. Particularly when she saw a beautiful woman going in or out of Clay's office. And there were many. Business or personal, she could never tell.

Well, Cindy told herself, his women were not her concern. And she didn't care, she told herself, how many women he squired around town. Or which one "got hold" of him. From the women she could see drifting through his office, there were many contestants.

One of them drifted into *her* office.

"A Ms Denise Salter to see you," said Cindy's secretary.

"All right, Ann. Show her in," Cindy replied while she wondered, Salter? Why did that name sound familiar? Salter... Oh, yes! Salter Demolition Company. They'd sent in an unbelievably low bid on demolishing the shopping area. But *Ms* Salter?

"It was my father's company," explained the exotic redhead, who was wearing only a shade too much carefully applied makeup. "You see, he died recently." The incredibly long lashes fluttered in apparent grief. "I'm determined to keep his company alive, Ms Rogers. In his memory."

"You're managing the company now?" Cindy asked.

"Oh, yes. But more than managing. I work right along with the guys, just like Dad did."

"Oh." Cindy tried to reconcile this fact with the lashes and the long enameled nails. "Well, all the bids aren't in yet. So we haven't made a decision."

"Yes. That was what Mr. Kencade said. He's been so helpful and he told me to come in and talk to you. You see, when I explained how much the job meant—you know, about my father and keeping the company alive—Mr. Kencade said my bid was extremely low for the type of job it is."

"And you want to change your bid?" Cindy asked. "Did you want your copy back, or should I just cancel—"

"I don't know what to do. I plan to see Mr. Kencade again so he can advise me. He said I should make another appointment because he's frightfully busy this morning. He said we were a small company, you know, and with such a big job... Well, if I took it on, I'd have to hire more men and probably get more equipment. Or maybe he could arrange it so my company would be assigned to just a portion of the work. That's what he suggested, anyway. And he told me to alert you about this—until I have a chance to talk to him again and get his advice. This is all so new to me, you see, and sometimes I feel so helpless."

About as helpless as a clawing cat, Cindy thought. *And you can just save those fluttering eyelashes for Clay.* She stood up to signal that the interview was over.

"Then I won't make any decision about this until I talk to Mr. Kencade. Thank you for coming in, Ms Salter."

Ten minutes later Cindy barged into Maggie's office and, finding her alone, asked, "Is this Ms Denise Salter for real?"

Maggie looked up from her desk and sniffed. "Oh, she's for real all right."

"But . . . a demolition expert? It just doesn't go with all that . . . that . . ." Cindy waved a hand in a gesture that so aptly described Denise's appearance that Maggie laughed out loud.

"Left over from the beauty parlor where she worked before deciding to take over her late father's business. A decision she made, I'm sure, the instant she tumbled into the powerful arms of Clay Kencade."

"Oh, then she—" Cindy's heart sank "—she's close to Clay?"

"No, dear. She hardly knows him."

"But you said . . ." Cindy's relief gave way to a twinge of anger. "Maggie, you're not making sense!"

"You think not? Listen to this." Maggie tapped the desk with her pencil. "Daniel Salter, of Salter Demolition, was a widower and definitely on the outs with his only daughter, Denise. In fact, or so Tom was told by one of Dan's workers, they hadn't been in touch for more than three years. But then Dan had a heart attack and fell from a scaffold. When he was rushed to the hospital, they, of course, called Denise. Because the accident occurred on one of Clay's projects, they called him, too. So he trots right over to the hospital, showing up just in time to comfort the poor weeping bereaved daughter. And our little Denise is no fool. She knows when she's got a prizewinning ticket."

"Ticket?"

"A floundering business, Mr. K.'s specialty."

"Oh, yes." Cindy nodded thoughtfully. "And a dead father."

"Right you are. Mr. K. would certainly have mentioned his own father's heart attack. And she's got another thing in her favor." Maggie leaned back in her chair and smiled wickedly. "She's a woman and oh-so-very helpless," she added in an excellent mimicry of Denise's soft, breathless voice. "I think it's a hangover from his stepsisters," Maggie added. "One of his mother's husbands had three girls who absolutely idolized him. And it was during his most impressionable adolescent period. Ever since, he's seen himself as the great protector of womankind!"

"Patsy is more like it!" Cindy snorted. She leaned across the desk. "You know, Maggie, Clay's mother did him a real disservice—providing him with so many step-siblings. Which reminds me, didn't you say something about Clay supporting a home for troubled boys, one that had been so much help to one of his stepbrothers?"

Maggie nodded.

"None of this appears in any of his tax records."

Maggie spread out her hands. "I wouldn't know about that."

"Well, I intend to find out," Cindy said. "Call me when he gets back to the office, will you?"

Two hours later Maggie called, and Cindy went into Clay's office and found him standing by the window. She approached the subject directly.

"It's come to my attention, not from you, of course, that through the years you've given some financial support to a home for troubled boys. Is this true?"

"Well, er, yes," he answered, throwing her a startled look. Much like a small boy caught with his hand in the cookie jar, she thought. "You see, I knew a boy once who got into a bit of trouble. And the man in charge of this home really impressed me. He was able—"

"Never mind the details. What's the name of the place?"

"Bolsten's Ranch. It's a few miles upstate. The man started out pretty much on his own. Now I think he gets some county help and some funds from the United Way."

"And from you." She faced him, her hands in her jacket pockets, and demanded, "How much? And for how long?"

He frowned down at her. "I don't know. Maybe fifteen years, or..." He ran a hand through his hair. "Look, Cindy, I don't know how long or how much. You wouldn't expect me to keep a record, would you?"

"Oh, of course not," she answered, her mouth twisting with sarcasm. "Couldn't be more than a million or two." She sighed. "And we can only go back three years."

"What are you talking about?"

"Taxes, Clay. Carruthers and Cranston have been doing both your corporate and your personal taxes for several years. And I've never seen a listing of even one charitable donation."

"Because I prefer a gift to be a gift, not a tax loophole."

"That's a most unusual attitude."

"I know. I'm supposed to squeal about high taxes and work hard to avoid paying them. The more taxes I pay means the more money I'm making, and I don't mind giving the government its share. How can a country operate without taxes? Besides I owe." He glanced out of the window and then turned back to her. "It was government money that got my father out of a jam."

"Oh? I heard it was you who got your father out of a jam."

"You must have been talking to Tom or Maggie." He smiled. "They're prejudiced. No, Cindy. When my father had the first attack, we were broke. Stone broke. He spent two weeks in the charity ward of the county hospital—

getting the best care, I might add. And then, well, he'd already lost the business, which, thank goodness, was incorporated. But he was about to lose the building he owned. I went to a lawyer who helped me get a small-business loan from the federal government. That was what enabled us to remodel the building and start Kencade Enterprises." He walked over to his desk, then walked back to her. "And let's not mention the student loans that helped pay my way through college. I think we've got a great country, Cindy. And when I pay taxes, I'm just giving back a little of what I owe. I don't mind paying them."

Cindy stood for a moment, arrested by the sincerity in his expression and her own feeling of unbounded admiration for this man, who was so different from any other man she'd ever encountered, either in or out of business. In her special field, accounting, each client invariably wanted to make as much money as possible and keep as much of it as he could. But this man . . .

She reached out and touched his arm. "I'm beginning to see the light," she said, unable to prevent the little catch in her voice. "But truly, it amazes me how you've managed to succeed despite the utter stupidity with which you operate." She pointed to the sofa. "Sit down. We need to talk."

"About what?" he asked, slanting an amused smile her way. But he took a seat as requested.

"About challenge and charity and getting on the same wavelength with your acquisitions analyst. And about how you could be a hell of a lot better off if you took my advice."

"Sounds like quite a conversation."

"No conversation. I talk. You listen."

He started to speak, but she held up a hand.

"You hired me to help you. And now that I know what you're really all about, I'm going to. So listen. Okay?"

He nodded, still looking amused. He was quiet while she took a little turn about the room, trying to organize her thoughts. Then she stopped and gazed down at him.

"The first thing we're going to do is take your charity out of the closet." Silencing him with a gesture, she continued, "A charitable donation is a legal deduction, not a loophole. We're going back three years and amending your tax returns. We just might get a big fat refund—which we sorely need. Because," she added, again raising her hand to stop him from speaking, "it takes money to run a charitable institution. Yes, charity—buying up defunct businesses and turning them into profit-making ventures that will save people's jobs, so they can support their families. And so they can pay their taxes like good little citizens to keep their country alive and kicking!" Pausing for breath, she rolled her eyes at him. "Very funny, huh? Well, my friend, that is an act of charity, whether you admit it or not."

Unable to check the laughter, he could only shake his head.

"So we're going to get back at least some of that charity money you dished out. And we're going to take this money from the sale of the shipping line and put it into T-bills, I think, and some other money markets. That way, it can be earning us a little more money while we intermittently parcel it out to the demolition companies and developers and engineers who are going to change all these decrepit companies—and keep the economy going. And we're going to hold off for a minute on buying until we can—"

"Okay, okay," he said. "I get your point."

"Do you really?" she asked, bending down to face him. "Are you listening? Because I really am on your wavelength. And I do want you to continue doing what you're doing. But I don't want you to go broke. I want you to stay afloat. Not just for your own good, but for the good of a lot of people. And, yes, for this fine country of which you're so all-fired proud!"

Now they were both laughing and he stood up.

"Okay, Cindy, I do get your point. I'm in your hands. Do with me what you will." His arms went around her, but he quickly drew back. "Oh, I'm sorry. I didn't mean—"

"It's okay," she said, a little breathless, aching to be in his arms again. She lowered her face, not wanting him to know. "We *can* work together," she said. "I do have your best interests at heart."

During the following weeks a beautiful working relationship developed between them. Cindy found she liked sharing Clay's visions. He was always thinking ahead. Even before demolition of the shopping area had begun, he was leasing space to prospective tenants and allowing them to consult with the architect about the design of their particular space. Conversion of the Denver tool plant had begun. A packaging engineer was in charge of new machinery being installed, while at the same time the employees were being retrained to produce the new tamperproof containers for medicines and foods. Cindy found she enjoyed handling the money and credit, a detail Clay hated. She enjoyed keeping pace with his ideas, which she found fascinating. She loved being on the same wavelength with Clay, and tried to close her mind to the fact that it was a strictly business relationship.

His women, she again told herself, were not her concern. And she tried to deny the tormented sensation that burned through her every time she saw him lunching in the executive dining room or leaving the building with some beautiful woman, most frequently Lisa Daniels or Denise Salter. It was hard, but Cindy kept her lips buttoned when Clay decided to let the Salter company have one portion of the demolition contract. "Salter's daughter is having a real struggle trying to get the company going again," he'd confided to Cindy—who was hardly surprised.

When Denise continued to parade in and out of Clay's office, Cindy couldn't help asking Maggie, "What does she want now? She's already got the contract!"

"Oh, don't be naive, honey," Maggie said, opening wide, knowing eyes. "You don't think *that* was what she wanted! No, Cindy, that's just her ticket into Clay's office and, she hopes, his heart. And I must say our Ms Salter is on the right track. One way to get Mr. K.'s attention is to ask for his advice."

"Oh, I see," said Cindy, biting her lip.

"And she's got all the trappings—a floundering business, a dead father to commemorate, and she's *so* helpless! And rather pretty in spite of all that makeup," Maggie said, adding significantly, "you know men!"

"Yes," Cindy snapped. "They're idiots!"

Maggie smiled as Cindy flounced out.

CLAY WAS KEEPING his promise. But it was killing him. It was hard to sit across from a vibrant enthusiastic Cindy at the conference table, to watch her lovely flushed face and still resist the impulse to go around and take her in his arms and kiss those delicately curving lips. And he was absolutely fascinated by her efficiency—the way she managed to balance the figures and keep his cash and credit flowing so that he was never impeded from doing the things he wanted to do. That is, unless she issued a flat "No, we can't do that!" Funny the way she'd straighten her shoulders and throw back her head to face him! Small and yet . . . so firm.

And so damned appealing!

But she'd set the rules . . . business only. And if there was going to be any change, she'd have to make the first move. He wouldn't get his signals crossed again.

And though he had a hard time keeping his mind off Cindy, at least he found himself constantly busy, both during and after office hours. Lisa was always coming up with something interesting to do—tennis, the theater, a party on her yacht. She had completely forgiven him for neglecting her in Denver, and had even persuaded her cousin to throw a celebration party when the Denver plant reopened.

Clay still went to Greenwich to practice with Johnny, but he stayed out of Cindy's way when he did so.

CINDY STOOD at Johnny's bedroom window and looked down at Clay and the children. Clay had a bucket of balls that he was pitching to Johnny. He kept Jamey and Teri well out of range, but allowed them to participate by collecting the balls and refilling the empty bucket. Their laughter and chatter floated up through the open window. Cindy felt very lonely.

She turned away from the window to pick up Johnny's blue school pants and put his white shirt in the hamper. He should have done it himself, but he'd been in a rush because Clay had come. And after dinner he'd have his homework.

Should she ask Clay to dinner? But even when she asked, he never stayed these days. Indeed, after the hour or so of play when the children ran in, she would hear the soft purr of Clay's departing car. Was he avoiding her?

What makes you think you're even on his mind, Cindy Rogers? He's probably rushing off to meet one of his many ladies.

Cindy went downstairs, reflecting that she was letting her own life become too narrow—completely centered around the children and work. She ought to get out more. Maybe Maggie would accompany her to the theater one night. And she'd been meaning to call Jane and some of the others from her old office—they could have lunch or something.

When she entered the family room, the kids were running in and... Her breath caught, her heart thumped and she only dimly heard Jamey say, "Here's Clay. Can he eat with us, Cindy? Can he?"

Clay smiled and shook his head. "You kids go and wash up. I want to talk to your aunt. Come outside a minute, Cindy?"

Probably only business, Cindy thought, but she couldn't stop the wild beating of her heart as she followed him through the open garage.

"The kids," he said, as they reached the outside driveway. "Johnny and Teri are giving Jamey a hard time."

"Oh, dear. Again?" She sighed. Those two had been calling Jamey "fraidy-cat" ever since he'd stopped the swimming lessons. "The little monsters! I've told them and told them—"

"Kids say whatever's on their minds, however brutal."

"You're right. I've told Jamey not to pay any attention to them."

"I guess the sticks and stones idea is okay." He rubbed his fist against his chin. "But there's something more important here. Sometimes a boy needs to prove himself. And... well, every kid ought to learn how to swim."

"But he's terrified of the water," she said. "Johnny swims like a fish and Teri's too young to be scared." She bit her lip. "Jamey should have started when he was younger. But that was just at the time his mother...well, you know. And I don't want to push him now."

"No." Clay regarded her with such warmth that Cindy blushed. "You just want to protect him. But what I was going to say is, what if I take him over to my club a few times? With no kids to harass him, and with me along, he just might risk a few strokes. What do you say?"

"You'd be willing to do that?" She paused, trying to digest the certain knowledge that Clay cared about the kids. He'd never desert them, even if—

"Sure. Why not?" He looked at his watch. "Gotta go, Cindy. I'll pick him up Sunday after my golf game. About two. Okay?"

She nodded and he was off before she could thank him.

On Sunday the other two kids clamored to go along.

"No," Clay said firmly. "This is Jamey's time. You have baseball, Johnny. And—" he reached down to pick up Teri "—how about the zoo for you, little lady?"

"Today?" cried Teri.

"Not today, but soon. That is, if Cindy approves. Just you and me."

"And I can see the monkeys and have puffy candy?"

"Monkeys and puffy candy." Clay laughed as he set her down. "Come on, Jamey."

Jamey looked very smug sitting beside Clay in the Jaguar. And Cindy felt as bereft as Teri and Johnny did as they watched the car move slowly down the driveway.

She told herself it was to cheer up the children that she decided to have dinner ready when the two returned.

"We'll make a special man's dinner," she said to Johnny and Teri. "And not the usual steak and potatoes, either."

Something a little out of the ordinary. Something Clay would like. She remembered that her dad had been so pleased with the corned beef and cabbage dinner Claire had once fixed for his birthday.

Anybody who can read can cook, she told herself as she searched frantically through Claire's cookbooks for the recipe. And found it!

They rushed to the store to buy everything they'd need. Then she told the children, who were as excited as she, to set the table while she prepared the food. "In the dining room with candles and flowers and everything. Of course you can help, Teri. Johnny will show you were to place the knives and forks."

While the beef simmered she prepared the vegetables, which were to be cooked separately and placed around the corned beef on the large round serving platter.

She would do everything just as Claire had done. "Drain meat, stud with whole cloves and bake twenty minutes, glazing with sauce." She measured carefully for the sauce: two tablespoons water...two teaspoons vinegar...one-quarter cup corn syrup...dry mustard... Did they have it? She searched the spice cabinet. Oh yes...one teaspoon dry mustard, one-quarter teaspoon allspice. Okay!

At five o'clock, when Clay had said they'd be back, dinner was almost ready. The salads were on the table, the vegetables timed just right, the meat ready to be sliced. She would wait until they arrived to pop the corn muffins into the oven and steam the cabbage.

Just time enough for Clay to have a drink and relax.

When she heard the car in the driveway, she gasped. A lump swelled in her throat and she could hardly breathe.

"Cindy, I can swim now...I almost can!" Jamey shouted as he bounded into the family room.

"He did a few strokes," added Clay, following more sedately behind. He smiled at Cindy. "I think he'll make it after a few more sessions."

"Clay let me ride on his back and we swam across the whole pool. Twice! And I wasn't scared."

"Great, Jamey!" Cindy gave him a hug.

"We fixed dinner," said Johnny.

"Table all pretty. Come see," Teri urged, grasping one of Clay's fingers.

"I thought you two swimmers might be hungry," Cindy offered. "So I . . . we . . . fixed dinner."

"And I know just what you fixed!" Clay's eyes lighted as he paused to enjoy the savory aroma drifting from the kitchen. "Corned beef with... Gosh, it takes me back. My aunt Marilyn used to fix it like that, some kind of special sauce with syrup and allspice and I don't know what else."

His eyes questioned her and she nodded.

"I thought you couldn't cook!"

"I can read," she said, giving him a smug look.

"And very well from what I can see. I sure wish I could stay. But I'm sorry, Cindy. I already have a dinner engagement. And I can't very well change it. I made it a month ago."

She hardly heard his explanations and apologies, was only vaguely aware of Johnny's argument with Jamey ("riding on Clay's back isn't swimming!") or of Teri, who still urged Clay to "see the table."

Somehow she managed to smile, to murmur, "Oh, it's quite all right. It's nothing. I had to fix dinner for the kids, anyway." She was relieved he hadn't seen the table.

Then he was gone.

She had to throw out most of the cabbage. The kids wouldn't eat it.

Did he really have another engagement?

Silly woman. Of course he did!

With whom?

Not that it mattered. After all, the dinner tonight had been nothing special. Just a gesture of appreciation for all Clay was doing for Johnny and Jamey.

CHAPTER ELEVEN

IT WAS THE LAST GAME of the season, between the Semco Cubs and the most formidable of all their rivals, the team they hadn't yet been able to beat—the Pizza Pirates.

The game had reached a crucial moment. It was the bottom of the last inning and the score was 20 to 18 in favor of the Pirates. Johnny's team, the Cubs, still had a chance. They were at bat with two men on base and only one out. Cindy, coaching Todd on second, grinned when she saw that Davey Prescott was the next batter. He was their best. If anybody could bring in the two runs, Davey could.

There was a pause for time out while the Pirates' coach, Bob Bailey, sent in a new pitcher. Davey struck out. Cindy's spirits sagged and she felt for the boy, who left the plate disheartened. She saw Steve briefly put an arm around his son. She couldn't hear what he said but she knew it was a reassuring "it's okay, Davey." Steve Prescott was a good father, she thought. Then she felt her stomach tighten with apprehension as she realized who the next batter would be. Johnny.

Oh, no. He'll feel under so much pressure. He's so sensitive, and if he strikes out now he'll never get over it. The last out—their last chance! He'll feel he's to blame if—

She held her breath as she saw Johnny walk up and tap his bat to the plate in a very professional manner, then she let out her breath and yelled, "Come on, Johnny! You can do it!'' *Please,* she prayed. *Just let him make a hit. Just one.*

She tried to calm herself. This was ridiculous. It was only a game, not his whole life. *Please don't let him strike out!* The pitcher wound up and she shut her eyes.

She heard the resounding whack as Johnny's bat connected on the very first pitch, and her eyes flew open to see the ball skim far out into left field. Far, far out of reach! A home run!

Cindy couldn't contain herself. She jumped up and down, clapping her hands and yelling with pride as the three boys loped around the bases to score. *We won! We won—21 to 20.* And it was Johnny who did it!

She ran up, wanting to throw her arms around her nephew and congratulate him. She couldn't get near him. He was surrounded by his teammates, who were jumping up and down and cheering.

Then, through the hubbub, Cindy heard the voice of Bailey, the Pizza Pirates' coach. ''Prescott,'' he said in a tone of righteous indignation, ''I want to challenge that run!''

''You what?'' Steve looked at him in surprise. ''Are you trying to say it was a foul ball? You saw it yourself. It went almost straight past second and out into left field. And you say—''

''No, not a foul. The boy was batting contrary to Little League rules.''

''What?''

''He didn't have his helmet on.''

Steve, like almost everyone else, turned to look at Johnny, who was still wearing his baseball cap, pushed back on his head.

"Oh," said Steve. "I guess I didn't notice." He turned back to Bailey. "For Pete's sake, surely you don't want to discount the hit just because—"

"It's a hard-and-fast rule, Prescott."

The crowd suddenly quieted as the challenge was issued. Parents and other onlookers had come down from the bleachers and stood in a circle around the two coaches. They all seemed to hold their breath as Steve asked, "You mean you're asking for a replay?"

"No. I want you to forfeit the game to the Pirates."

Cindy gasped and everyone began to talk at once. Bob Bailey, she thought hotly, was the kind of coach who gave Little League a bad name. One reason the Pirates were consistent winners was that he kept the best players in the field while the other boys stayed on the bench. He wasn't like Steve, who always made sure each boy got a turn. But Bailey evidently cared nothing about the boys. Only about winning. And now he wanted to take from Johnny what he had worked so hard to achieve. Well, she wouldn't let him!

"You can't do that!" she said, stepping between the two men. "It's your fault, too. If you saw he didn't have his helmet on, why didn't you stop your pitcher from pitching?" She hardly heard what the man said or what she retorted. She only knew that she was fighting mad, and she wouldn't let this beefy-faced man take away Johnny's victory.

"Wait a minute," said Steve, trying to restore order. "Let's not let this get out of hand. After all, it's the kids' game."

For the first time, Cindy turned to glance at the boys. Many were hanging around listening to the argument. But just as many had deserted to toss a few balls and play with one another.

Steve's voice rose above the crowd. "Listen, let's allow the boys to make the decision. We'll have the players, Pirates and Cubs, take a vote on whether the play, and the score, should stand."

Cindy saw Bob Bailey smile. "Sure. That's fair," he said.

Cindy felt the hot blood rush to her face. Of course. He knew there were more players on the Pirates' team. She moved forward, wanting to bash Bailey with her fists.

"No!" she shouted. "That's not fair. I won't let you—"

"Cindy." Someone grasped her arm, but she pulled loose.

"Leave me alone!" she shouted.

"Come on, Cindy." Clay pulled her gently but firmly away from the crowd.

"No!" she protested. "Let me go. I want to tell them—"

"I know what you want to tell them. But not now. You're much too excited. Calm down. Steve's right. It is the kids' game." By this time he'd managed to get her over to the other side of the park.

"It's not fair!" she said, almost in tears. "Johnny hit that ball and—"

"Wasn't it a beaut?" Clay slammed his fist into his palm. "Whack! Over and gone at just the right time. Nobody, Cindy, nobody can take that away from him."

"But they *are* taking it away! Don't you see? There are more kids on the Pirates and you know they'll vote for themselves."

"You think the kids won't be as fair as you hotheaded adults?" He went on to tell her that she should give the boys more credit. And that she couldn't sugarcoat life for her nephew. "He has to take the lumps and go by whatever the kids decide. Like Steve said, it's their game. And no matter what they decide, nobody will ever forget that hit. Especially Johnny. No way can anybody take that from him.''

Cindy was calmer, but not reconciled when they returned to the group. The boys from both teams were seated in the bleachers and supplied with little slips of paper on which they were to scribble "yes," to honor the runs, or "no," not to do so. Cindy held her breath as the bits of paper were collected and counted.

She saw Steve smile, saw Bob Bailey shove his hands into his pockets and shrug. Every vote except two said "yes."

Now the tears did run down her cheeks as Cindy cheered with the others. "I'm so surprised," she said to Steve, and to Clay, standing beside her. "I thought...oh, I feel so ashamed. I really thought they'd be unfair.''

Steve shook his head. "No. They know how it feels to hit a home run. They wouldn't let Johnny down.''

Cindy squeezed Clay's hand and whispered, ''Thank you.''

The incident didn't seem to taint the great win, and the boys were in high spirits as they helped load the equipment into Steve's van. They were all eager to leave for the end-of-season swimming party that Steve was giving for all his players and their parents.

Cindy heard Johnny say, ''Can I ride with you, Clay? You're coming, aren't you? You don't have to go somewhere else, do you?''

She felt a little thrill of pleasure when Clay answered, ''Sure. Wouldn't miss it for anything. This is our big day.''

Cindy, following the map Marcy had circulated, was surprised to find that the Prescotts' house wasn't far from where she lived. But more spacious, she decided, as she turned up the curving driveway. It must be about six acres, she thought, looking at the beautiful landscaping and the many tall trees.

There was an Olympic-size swimming pool, and soon all the kids and many of the adults were diving in. Cindy, seeing Jamey dive in fearlessly with the rest, felt the same glow of pride she'd felt for Johnny when his bat struck that ball. And an overwhelming gratitude to Clay. In just three trips to his club he'd accomplished what weeks of swimming lessons had not.

She looked across at Clay who, along with one of the fathers, had been drafted by Steve to serve as lifeguards. Clad in a pair of Steve's trunks, he stood at one end of the pool, his wet body glistening in the late-afternoon sun, tall and lean and sinewy. Even across the pool Cindy could sense the strength and the caring with which his alert eyes scanned the swimmers. She liked the way he cared. And the way he instantly participated—and enjoyed the moment.

Enjoy the moment. He was right. Johnny's home run and Jamey's swimming were due almost entirely to just a little time spent with Clay. And at this moment... She watched him keeping a careful eye on Teri, who seemed determined to attempt anything that Ginger did. And Ginger was cavorting like a little fish, born to the water. Ginger and Davey, she thought, were great kids. And lucky to have such warm, understanding parents. Cindy remembered how Steve had slipped an arm around his son when Davey had been distraught over his strikeout. And Marcy was always so gracious, so supportive and easygoing.

And pregnant! Cindy glanced over to see Marcy setting plates on one of the picnic tables, one hand held to her back. *Working like that, while I stand here daydreaming.* She went quickly to the picnic area, a little distance from the pool, where Marcy and some other parents were arranging salads, baked beans, plates and cups on long tables. Steve was laying hot dogs and hamburgers on a large stone grill.

The party was fun. People finally emerged from the pool to eat, then formed into groups to talk or play games. Cindy was reminded of the gatherings in her own home when she was a child. This was a more opulent setting, of course, but similar. A family affair. Good-natured and relaxed.

We ought to do more things like this, she thought, as she gave Johnny a grocery bag and told him to collect the empty soda cans. *Whoever comes into my life or the children's we should enjoy together. I could invite Maggie out and she could bring her grandchildren.*

And Clay. He'd been good for the kids. Not like Dan.

No. That wasn't fair to Dan. He'd been good for them, too. He'd played with them, helped them forget. They had needed that at the time. It was just that Dan had left her— and them.

Enjoy the moment.

Clay was different from Dan. Yes, he played with the children, but he also...instructed. She knew that the children had grown a little stronger because of the moments Clay had spent with them. *And so have I,* she admitted, thinking of the incident at the game. And she was grateful.

Cindy was stuffing paper plates into a garbage bag when Steve caught her arm. "Cindy, would you take Marcy around to the patio and make her sit? She's been on her feet too long."

"Sure," Cindy said with a laugh. "For if she sitteth, so canst I. Put that platter down, Marcy, and come on, Marcy. I want to talk to you anyway."

"Go ahead, honey," Steve urged, giving his wife a quick kiss. "Clay and I will finish up."

Clay. He was still here. *And I like his being here,* she thought. She reveled in the sound of his voice calling to Johnny and Davey to quit horsing around until they cleared off that last table.

Almost everyone else had gone, and Cindy checked on Teri and Jamey, pleased to find them playing some kind of game with Ginger. Then she followed Marcy to the patio that surrounded the pool.

"What did you want to talk about?" asked Marcy, as she lowered her heavy body into one of the lounge chairs.

"Everything. But would you like me to get you a cold drink or something first?" she asked anxiously. Marcy did look a little tired.

"No. For goodness' sake, you're as bad as Steve. Sit down, Cindy. I'm fine. Now what is this *everything* you want to talk about?"

"Well..." Cindy started with the usual pleasantries, "Such a great party...Steve's a great coach...good season." Marcy responded in kind. Then something about the atmosphere suddenly touched Cindy. The men and children talking and laughing in the background. Sitting with Marcy while the giant trees cast shadows as the golden sun sank slowly behind them and bestowed a final glow on the still waters of the pool. She felt a sense of real companionship and could ask without hesitation what she really wanted to know. "How do you do it?"

"Do what?" Marcy asked, smiling.

"Manage your children so beautifully. And so easily. You never seem to worry."

"Oh, I worry all right. Everyone does."

"Not as much as I do." Cindy frowned. "Like right now. Yesterday I got a letter from the children's grandparents—the Atwoods—inviting the kids to spend the whole month of August with them." The letter had surprised and rather dismayed her. Now she found herself telling Marcy how John's parents had never really been interested in his kids. "I'm not sure it would be good for them to spend so much time with them."

Marcy chuckled. "I know just how you feel. I've got a sister in California who's a real dingbat. But I let her keep Ginger and Davey last summer when Steve and I went to Japan. The children survived—and actually enjoyed it. They do, you know," she said, looking at Cindy. "Survive, I mean."

"I know. I guess I'm always so anxious about doing the right thing. Because I'm not their real mother. I'm just their aunt."

"Yes, I know. Still, you're more related to your kids than I am to mine. I'm just a step-aunt."

"What?" Cindy sat up. "What do you mean, you're just a step-aunt?"

"I became one when I married Steve," Marcy explained as Cindy stared in surprise. She told how the children's parents, good friends of hers, were suddenly drowned in a boating accident when Davey was about five and Ginger three. Because there was no record of a surviving relative, the children were placed in the custody of child welfare, where Marcy, a social worker, was assigned the case. At her own request. She finally tracked down an uncle—Steve Prescott. "And I fell head over heels in love with Steve and married him. Four years ago."

"And you're still head over heels! But I'd given you credit for at least ten years," Cindy said, still trying to comprehend the situation. "I thought, of course, that you were their natural parents. Why, all those times we had lunch together, Marcy, you've never mentioned this."

"I guess I never thought about it. After a while, you just begin to feel you *are* the natural parent."

"And they call you Mom and Dad."

"That's a recent innovation. Davey's—on account of the baby." Marcy touched the bulge under her sundress. "It was Marcy and Steve until Davey decided on the Mom and Dad bit so the baby would get the nomenclature right. Actually, I think Davey wanted to be more like his peers. And whatever Davey decides, Ginger follows."

"I see," Cindy said, still trying to take it all in. "So Steve is really their uncle." *Like I'm an aunt,* she thought.

Marcy nodded and chuckled. "And you wouldn't believe how hard I fought to keep him from getting the children. I thought he seemed too unstable."

"Unstable! Steve Prescott?" Cindy exclaimed.

"You see how wrong first impressions can be?" Marcy said. "He didn't even have a permanent residence at the time and I thought—"

She never finished what she thought, for at that moment they were joined by Steve and Clay, who handed them tall frosty drinks and sat down to talk with them.

Or rather with each other. It seemed that Steve and Clay knew each other slightly because they were on some board together. The two of them were soon engaged in a mild disagreement about the policies of that board. So Cindy and Marcy continued their own conversation.

Then they were interrupted by Ginger, who wanted to know if she could take Teri down to the stable for a ride on her pony.

Steve said okay, but that he'd better go, too. "He's a very gentle pony," he assured Cindy.

They all walked down to the paddock and watched the children ride for a short time. Finally Clay helped Cindy pile the three Atwood children into the station wagon.

Cindy hoped for a wild moment that he would suggest following them home. But he didn't.

"Good night. Drive carefully" was all he said. He watched as they drove out, then got into his own car and turned in the other direction.

The beautiful day was over.

But not forgotten. Steve and Marcy—uncle and aunt. No, step-aunt. Almost in the same position as Cindy. Except that they had each other.

But not at first. And he had seemed . . . unstable? Steve Prescott? She couldn't believe it.

Clay was stable. He was living in the same place he'd lived when he was ten.

Clay. He had been there for the game. And for the party. It was like . . . well, two couples sitting together and—

Careful, Cindy!

Oh, my goodness, it's not as if I'm trying to promote anything. I'm just . . . well, I'm going to enjoy the moment and have fun with the people I like and the people the children like. I could have Marcy and Steve and the children over one Sunday. And Clay. Why not? He and Steve like each other.

And maybe . . .

JUST THREE DAYS LATER Steve telephoned Cindy from the hospital. "It's a girl! Karen Louise Prescott." He sounded jubilant as he added, "She's beautiful and Marcy's fine. Everything went really well."

"I'm so happy for both of you," Cindy said, tears springing to her eyes. She sent flowers and congratulations, but decided to wait until the baby was a bit older before visiting. And certainly any social affairs she planned with the Prescotts would have to be delayed.

Cindy was surprised when three weeks later Marcy phoned to invite her to a christening party for the following Sunday. "I know it's short notice," she said, "but I wanted to have it before my mother leaves."

Cindy thought of asking Clay to accompany her. But he wasn't even in town. In fact, lately he'd been out of town more than he'd been in. He had spent two weeks in Europe negotiating the sale of Scandinavian Shipping Lines. Now he was in Denver and not due back at the office until Monday. Of course he'd probably be in town by the weekend and the party was on Sunday....

Anyway, she couldn't ask him—she didn't have his home number. Still, he'd probably be at the party, she thought, so she dressed very carefully and took pains styling her hopelessly curly hair and putting on makeup.

"Oh, my! You do look nice." Mrs. Stewart, who had returned from her sister's early to stay with the children, looked admiringly at Cindy's silk shirtwaist dress. "That golden yellow really highlights your hair. Makes you fairly sparkle! No, Teri!" She picked up the little girl just in time. "We don't want to get Cindy all messy. She's going to a party."

Even the boys paused in their game of catch to say, "You look pretty, Cindy."

So she felt good about herself as she drove away. But it was strange to be without the children on a sunny Sunday afternoon. Strange to be going unescorted to a party. Of course it wasn't a dance—just a christening party. Still, she felt very much alone.

She was greeted at the door by Davey, all spruced up and looking like a little man in his tailored suit and tie. And it was Ginger who introduced her to the baby.

"This is my little sister," Ginger said, bending protectively over the old-fashioned rocking cradle to smooth a crease from the beautiful white christening dress. "Her name is Karen."

"And she's absolutely adorable," Cindy said, looking down at the baby, who returned her gaze with wide blue eyes. "She's got your eyes, Marcy. Exactly the same shape. And with Steve's jet-black hair. What a combination! She's beautiful."

"Yes, isn't she," agreed Steve. "Look at her dimples!"

"Hush, Steve." Marcy playfully slapped his hand. "Let others admire. You just say thank you."

"You leave Steve alone. He has a right to be proud. And so have you." Cindy laughed as she said it, but she was so moved by Steve's open adoration of his whole family and Marcy's radiant happiness that her eyes misted over. She hugged them both. *There's so much love in this house,* she thought, *that it spills over and envelops you.* She didn't feel alone anymore as she chatted with Marcy's mother and some of the other guests.

But when Clay arrived, Cindy suddenly felt conspicuously alone. Because he was accompanied by the exquisite woman Cindy had seen leaving with him on one of his trips.

"Lisa Daniels," said Marcy as she introduced them. "Lisa's on the board of the Children's Home Society with me. And this is Cynthia Rogers, Lisa. She's affiliated with Kencade Enterprises."

"Oh, yes!" Lisa graciously extended her hand. "This is the first time we've been introduced, but I've seen you several times at Clay's office."

"Yes, many times," Cindy said and was able to get several polite remarks past the lump in her throat, including a brief cheerful greeting to Clay. She managed not to look at him during the rest of the afternoon.

But all the pleasure was gone. Even Marcy's comment as Cindy was leaving couldn't cheer her up. "I see Clay brought Lisa Daniels, but the woman he was watching all afternoon was Cynthia Rogers. I particularly noticed, Cindy. What's with you two?"

"Nothing's with us," Cindy declared. "We're just friends and . . . business associates. That's all."

And I must remember that, she told herself as she drove home. Clay was honoring their agreement to have a "strictly business" relationship. Why couldn't she?

CHAPTER TWELVE

CINDY HAD TO MAKE an immediate decision about whether to let the children visit their grandparents. Mrs. Atwood phoned to say that her husband would be in New York on business in a few days, and the children could fly back with him. She seemed pleased about seeing the children would have a good time. Later in the month the grandparents planned to drive up to Niagara Falls, maybe cross the border into Canada.·

Cindy said she'd have to check on some things and would call back the next day. She asked Maggie what she thought about it.

"Sounds like a nice trip for them," Maggie said. "What's the problem?"

Cindy hesitated. "Oh, they don't really know them that well."

"Their own grandparents? Then it's about time they got to know them, don't you think?"

"I'm not sure. They're not the kind of grandparents . . . well, they're not like you."

"People are different, Cindy, even grandparents. Don't worry. The kids will survive."

That's what Marcy said, Cindy thought. Still, she told Maggie how doubtful John's mother had been about taking the children when their mother died.

"Maybe she was just being honest," said Maggie, "recognizing that she was beyond the age for raising them. Children are a big responsibility."

"But why does she want them now?"

"A month isn't a lifetime, my dear. And evidently she does want to know them. And she wants them to know her. Don't be selfish."

Cindy asked the children if they wanted to go.

"Wow!" said Johnny. "Niagara Falls! I've seen pictures of it."

"Wow!" Jamey repeated. "I've never been on a plane. That would be neat."

"I want to go," said Teri.

Nothing about being sorry to leave or about missing her! Or about how she would miss them.

She let them go and gave Mrs. Stewart the month off. She had never felt so alone in her whole life!

Be careful what you wish for. You might get it. She grimaced at the old saying, one her mother always used to repeat. Had there really been moments, no matter how few, when she'd yearned to be back in her free before-the-children life with no timetables and no reason to hurry home? Had the children become so much a part of her that she couldn't be herself? Couldn't enjoy theaters and late dinners and dating?

Dating. Of course she'd had opportunities. But she was too busy and . . . not interested. In a rare moment of complete honesty she admitted to herself that the only man she wanted a date with was Clay Kencade. And Clay wasn't even around.

Clay was busy flying back and forth to Denver, making sure everything fell into place at Denver Tools, which was to have its grand opening next week, renamed Denver Packaging. The few times he did make brief appearances in the office, he was so busy that Cindy seldom saw him. She was quite surprised on Tuesday morning when he walked into her office and dropped a package on her desk.

"Just to say thank-you."

She caught her breath as she stared up at him and wondered if it would ever fade—the little glow she always felt in the presence of this handsome, virile man. He was so—

"Well, aren't you going to open it?"

She transferred her gaze to the packet, picked it up and slipped off the plastic cover. A stock certificate for one hundred shares in Denver Packaging!

"Oh, Clay!" She was overwhelmed.

"You've been great, Cindy, the way you've managed the financing. The board members decided you deserved a bonus."

"Thank you. But I was just doing my job. I didn't expect this."

"Well, it's not worth that much now. But—" his face brightened with excitement "—hang on to those shares, kid. We've already got a big contract with a leading medical supply house and several others pending. I've got to go. See you later." He was gone before she could say anything else.

The glow became a steady warmth, and suddenly Cindy felt her eyes mist with tears. Board members nothing! It was Clay... wonderful, generous Clay. *Hang on to those shares, kid.* As if she could ever let them go. This link between them, however small, was something that made her a part of him.

Not him, you idiot! Just Kencade Enterprises. And don't start feeling so special, either. This is the kind of thing he does for all his associates.

She put the stock certificate away and went back to work.

Cindy was about to leave the office on Wednesday afternoon when Maggie buzzed. "Come in here a minute, please, Cindy."

She hurried in to find Maggie sitting at her desk and Tom perched on one corner of it complacently chewing the end of his pipe.

"I want you to do me a favor, honey," Maggie said. "I really goofed. I somehow missed putting these papers in with Clay's things before he left. It's important that he have them right away. Would you take them to him for me?"

"To Denver?" Cindy was puzzled. What kind of papers couldn't just be delivered? "Couldn't you send them by express?"

"No. I hate to use even a courier," Maggie said. "This is rather sensitive material and I don't want it to go astray or get into the wrong hands. I'd feel better if someone from the staff gave it personally to Mr. K."

"Oh." Cindy turned to Tom.

He coughed. "Don't look at me. I have to be here. They're starting on the 'Harry K.' project tomorrow." The shopping area was to be called the Harry K. Mall.

"You mean they're starting the demolition? Why do you have to be here for that?"

"Because he does," Maggie said. "Why are you stalling, Cindy? It would be a nice break for you. You could stay as long as you like. The kids are gone."

"Yeah," Tom interjected. "You said you were feeling lost, rattling around in that big house all by yourself."

"You just might enjoy it." Maggie pointed a pencil at her. "You could go to the celebration ball on Saturday that Lisa Daniels's bigwig cousin is giving."

"And you'd be there for the official opening on Monday," Tom added. "Nice for Clay if one of us was there."

"Anyway, you have to," Maggie said. "I don't see how—"

"All right," Cindy agreed. There was no reason she shouldn't go. "I might take an extra day or so and fly over to Phoenix to see my parents."

"Good." Maggie picked up the phone and quickly flipped through a directory. "I can get you a flight for to-morrow morning." By the time Maggie had made hotel and plane reservations and handed her the tightly sealed papers, Cindy was beginning to feel quite excited. It was a good time to get away. She'd never been to Denver and she was eager to see the renovated plant on which they'd all worked so hard.

And Clay. It wouldn't be like a date, but... Bergdorf Goodman was still open. If she was going to the celebration ball, she needed something to wear.

AT DENVER PACKAGING late Thursday afternoon, Clay sat in the president's office, going over some last-minute de-tails with Stevens. He was taken aback when Stevens's secretary buzzed to announce, "A Ms Rogers to see Mr. Kencade."

Stevens cocked a questioning eyebrow, but Clay felt too surprised to react. Cindy? Here? Stevens shrugged and told his secretary to show Ms Rogers in. Both men stood to greet her, and Clay saw Stevens's eyes light with admira-tion.

Cindy's trim figure was clad in a smart jumpsuit of tiny red and blue checks. It was open at the throat and had a wide stand-up collar, which emphasized the lovely curve of her neck. A blue leather bag was slung over her shoulder and she carried a sealed packet that she handed to Clay.

"I'm sorry to disturb you," she said, her apologetic nod including Stevens. "But Maggie said this was urgent and I was to hand it to you personally. So I thought I should come straight out to the plant."

"Thank you." Clay automatically accepted the packet, but could not take his gaze from Cindy. Her lovely flushed face, her forever tousled hair and those beautiful tempting lips. He heard Stevens cough and turned quickly. "Oh, yes, Jim, this is Cynthia Rogers. Cindy, Jim Stevens, president of Denver Packaging."

"How do you do?" she said, smiling and taking Stevens's outstretched hand.

"So you're the financial wizard Clay's been telling us about?"

"No, not really," she said, laughing. "I just try to keep pace with what's happening."

"Well, now, you must come and let me show you what's been happening here. Clay, why don't you just stay in my office and finish up, maybe relax a bit, and I'll show Ms Rogers around."

"Just a minute," Clay said, rather resenting Stevens's proprietary air. "You're not rushing back, are you, Cindy?" He smiled when she shook her head. "Good. You're registered at the Denvian? Good. I'll drive you back to the hotel when Stevens has finished showing off." He reluctantly watched them go. He would have liked to show her through the plant himself. But Jim was so proud, and of course it was really his plant.

Clay looked at the packet he still held. What the devil was Maggie sending him? It was so tightly sealed that he took some time to open it. When he did, all he found were several worthless printouts. What the hell!

There was a sealed note and he tore it open. In Maggie's precise handwriting he read, "When opportunity knocks, open the door. Were you surprised to see who walked in? Good luck, Maggie."

He couldn't help laughing out loud. Good, solid, dependable, meddling Maggie, who could always read him like a book! What she'd sent him was Cindy! A perfect opportunity—no children, no business. And no time like the present!

IT WAS GOOD, Clay thought, to have Cindy beside him as he drove back to the hotel.

"I think I'm beginning to appreciate you. Or maybe," she said, laughing, "I'm taking on some of Stevens's feelings."

"Oh, he's quite a guy, isn't he?" Clay said, speeding up a bit to pass a truck.

"Funny. That's exactly what he said about you."

"Oh?"

"Yes. He said he was really in a mess. He'd kept the tool plant going at a loss for a whole year just because he hated to put people out of work. But he knew he couldn't continue like that, and he was about to close the business and dump the facilities on the highest bidder. If anyone was even interested in bidding. And then," Cindy said in admiring tones, "somebody told him to talk to the great Clay Kencade. And presto chango! He declares that you're nothing less than a magician."

"Oh, come on, Cindy." Clay shot her a quick glance. "You're putting me on."

"I'm only quoting Mr. Stevens. Oh, Clay, he's so proud of the new plant and the fact that he's hiring instead of firing." She told how Stevens had taken her over every inch of the plant, all the while singing Clay's praises. "'Who would have thought,' he said, 'of changing from outmoded tools to tamperproof containers!' He thinks you're a genius!"

"Hardly." Clay laughed as he pulled into a parking lot at the hotel. "We're just following the old find-a-need-and-fill-it rule."

"Not we. You. Not everyone has the knack of recognizing what can be changed, or the wisdom and courage to risk doing it. You have both." Cindy reached over to touch his hand, still resting on the wheel. "As Stevens says, you're quite a guy."

This was new coming from Cindy, and it made him feel strangely embarrassed, though deeply pleased. He raised her hand to his lips. "Thank you," he managed. "Now, before you say something you might regret, let's go to dinner."

He wanted to prolong the dinner. He would have been happy just to sit and watch her, intrigued by the way the candlelight played on her smooth skin. She looked more delicate and ethereal than ever. Delicate she wasn't, he thought, remembering her bossy, businesslike stance each time she delivered a "No, we can't do that" ultimatum. But tonight she looked . . . fragile, defenseless and so utterly desirable that he ached to lift her in his arms and carry her up to his room and tuck her into bed. His bed.

"What are you thinking?" Cindy asked, smiling as she put down her coffee cup.

"About getting signals crossed."

"What?"

"Never mind. You've had a long day, what with the travel and the time change. I'd better take you to your room." Privately, he thought that he had four days in which to uncross those signals.

"I've got big plans for us tomorrow," he said as he opened the door to her room. "So meet me in the lobby at nine. And wear pants. It'll be a rough trip."

"Oh? Where are we going?"

"Mountain climbing," he answered, trying to still the desire that raced through him as he gazed at her lips. Better not risk it. "See you tomorrow," he said instead, and hastily departed.

When he met her in the lobby the next morning, Clay took one look at her flat sandals and herded her into one of the hotel shops. When they came out she glanced down at the jogging shoes she wore and the sweatshirt draped on her arm. "I feel overloaded," she said.

"You won't when we get where we're going."

"And just where *are* we going?" she asked as he helped her into the car.

"Mountain climbing."

"Clay!"

He chuckled. "All right. I won't make you climb it," he promised as he drove out of the parking lot. "Come to think, I've never heard it called a mountain. Just Red Rock. And sometimes Red Rock Amphitheater."

"A theater?" she asked. "On top of a mountain?"

"Not on top. *In.* Carved by nature. One of the natural phenomena of the world. I picked up a brochure, and you can read about it when we stop for brunch."

The roadside café he chose wasn't an ordinary one. The Treetop Inn was famous, she soon learned, because of the large cage in the center of the dining room housing a live tree and a number of colorful exotic birds.

"This is so beautiful. And so different," said Cindy, watching the flashes of color as the birds flitted among the branches. She felt special just being there with Clay. She leaned against the pale-green leather cushions and looked across at him. "Have you ever been here before?"

"Oh, yes, many times." She wondered if he sensed her letdown, for he quickly added, "But I've never been to Red Rock. I'm anxious to see it."

She remembered then to look at the brochure. It described the amphitheater as "a dramatic record of the ages. A majestic theatre pushed out of the ocean millions of years ago by the natural movements of earth and water."

"And I'd never heard of it," she said.

"Neither had I until I started coming to Denver. Like I'd never heard of Stone Mountain until I went to Georgia. Or of the Siebengebirge until I visited Germany."

"Guess I've never done much traveling," she said, looking at the scrambled egg on her plate. She suddenly felt very inexperienced. And rather dull.

"No traveling? Have you always been bogged down with your books and . . . other duties?"

"Oh, no," she said quickly. Goodness, she thought, had she been pulling the poor-little-me bit? "There was a time . . . Well, Dan had a boat, a fairly good-sized sloop, and we did quite a lot of sailing."

"Tell me."

"Oh, we didn't go far, of course. But we'd sail to interesting places like Nantucket, Martha's Vineyard, places like that."

"Not about the sailing. Tell me about him."

"Dan?" She saw that he'd pushed aside his plate and was regarding her intently. "What kind of person was he?"

She thought for a moment before she answered. "A fun person, I guess. He liked doing things. Not only the sailing, but going to the theater, late dinners, dancing..." This was the first time since their breakup that she'd talked at any length about Dan. Strange to be sharing it with Clay. "But he wasn't just fun," she concluded. "He was very helpful during my sister's illness and death. And then . . . well, I guess so much happened. It was inevitable that we . . . that he," she said honestly, "broke if off."

"And you miss him?"

"At first, well, there was a void. I felt deserted. But then, I was so busy with the children and all . . ."

"Yes, I can see that," Clay said, glancing at the check and placing several bills on the table. "I wonder if perhaps Dan felt deserted, too."

"Maybe," Cindy agreed. She was thoughtful as they left the restaurant and she remembered Dan's words about the children: "It's more like they've taken you."

Driving up the winding mountain road, they stopped once more at a vista point to look at the many-hued plains that stretched the sixteen miles back to Denver. Cindy was fascinated by the view.

But nothing could top her first sight of the theater itself. It was as if an unseen hand had taken a giant spoon and scooped out a portion of the mountain, creating a natural arena for the theater seats that sloped down toward the big flat rock that formed the stage. Tall sandstone rocks stood guard on either side, while another slanted backward from the stage like a huge Hollywood backdrop.

Cindy stood transfixed, enraptured as the rays of sun fell on the rocks and were reflected back in lavender, blue and all the colors of a rainbow. Clay seemed as silently awed as she, and Cindy reached for his hand, glad they were sharing this first view.

It felt almost as if they were sharing a private space, too, away from the rest of the world. Except for two other couples, who were obviously just as anxious to be alone, she'd seen no tourists. She commented on this absence to Clay.

"Probably because there's no performance tonight. And it's a weekday, not a holiday. I'm glad," he said, tucking a stray lock of hair behind her ear. "I like being here alone with you."

So do I, she thought, but was too shy to say it aloud. She began to talk enthusiastically about the theater, drawing Clay's attention to the fact that performances had been possible long before seats and artificial lighting were added.

"I'm glad they concealed all the mechanical features and used sandstone seats to preserve the natural setting," Clay said. He seemed equally excited that the work had been done by WPA and CCC workers.

"Those were job creation programs in the thirties, right?" asked Cindy.

Clay nodded, telling her how his father had talked about the great depression. About how the government had started the Works Progress Administration and the Civil ian Conservation Corps to get the economy going again. "Pop was just a boy," Clay said, "but he remembers what it was like with so many people jobless and homeless. He said Roosevelt turned things around, not by doling out charity, but by putting people to work."

"And that's what you do, isn't it?" Cindy said, reaching over to touch his hand. Every day she learned more about him, she thought. It was true that he was an excellent businessman. But what he really cared about was the people who worked for him. She felt a glow of pride as she looked up at him. "I'm glad to be a part of Kencade Enterprises," she said.

"Part of the company, but not of the man?" he asked softly.

"I—I don't know what you mean."

"I think you do. Why do you avoid me, Cindy?"

"I don't . . . not exactly." She stared down at the great sandstone backdrop.

He cupped her chin in his hand and turned her face gently toward him. "Is it because of that other man?" he asked, and she was surprised by the compassion in his eyes.

"Other man?" she asked.

"That fellow you were engaged to. Did he hurt you so badly?"

"Dan! Goodness, I never—" She stopped, hating to admit she'd never really loved the man she had once intended to marry. Not like— "No," she said. "Dan and I had some good times, but what I felt for him wasn't...isn't... Well, it wouldn't have worked. Dan and I weren't meant for each other."

"Then what are you afraid of, Cindy?"

Of you, she wanted to scream. *Because I could love you as I've never loved anyone else. And if you walked away...*

"Cindy?" he prompted, leaning toward her.

She was saved from replying by the rain that came then, not just a few drops, but all at once, in torrents. They ran, across the benches and over the dividers until they reached one of the ledges that jutted out from the rock wall. Huddled in a crevice, almost like a small cave, they were sheltered from the storm.

"Are you all right?" Clay asked, brushing the wet hair away from her face.

"I'm fine," she said, shaking out her sweatshirt and pulling it on. She laughed as she shivered. "You were right. I don't feel overloaded now."

"You're cold? Come here." He unzipped his weatherproof jacket and held it open, inviting her to share it with him.

She went willingly into his arms, snuggling against his chest and feeling the warmth of the jacket enclose them both.

"Is this better?" he asked, his lips against her forehead.

"Yes. Oh, yes." It was wonderful, like being in heaven. Feeling the beat of his heart under her cheek, hearing the rain splash and form into gulleys, breathing in the essence of the rain and fresh damp earth . . . and Clay.

"Oh, Cindy." His voice was a hoarse whisper and she felt his body tense as his lips met hers in a long, lingering kiss. A kiss so tender, so intoxicatingly sweet, that her whole body throbbed with wanting him. She wound her arms around his waist, slipped her hands under his sweater to caress the bare taut skin of his back and was filled with delight to hear him gasp. She traced light kisses along his chin and down his neck, let her tongue taste the salty hollow of his throat and reveled in his agonizing groan of pleasure.

She wanted to tantalize and please him. She wanted to surrender to the desires racing though her as his hands and lips possessively caressed her. She felt such a sense of certainty, of belonging...as if she were part of Clay, part of the rain that gushed and pounded against the rocks, part of the ocean that had existed more than a million years ago, churning, carving and changing.... And all at once she knew that everything changes...and nothing changes. And now is all we have, all that matters. She pressed closer to Clay, not wanting to lose this now, this magic moment of togetherness.

THE SWEET NEW FEELING of togetherness didn't end with the evening. It was still with her in the morning as she showered and donned a crisp lavender sundress and prepared to meet Clay. She felt sure that at last they were on the same wavelength. And it had nothing to do with business. It had to do with the intimate, exciting emotions they'd discovered the day before.

When she went down into the lobby and saw him coming to greet her, she knew he felt it, too. It was reflected in his dark eyes—warm, exultant, admiring. She hardly noticed other people. She was aware only of Clay and the exciting magnetic force that surrounded the two of them and drew them close.

Love? She caught her breath, not yet daring to call it by that name. She felt a prickle of delight as his hand closed over hers, and she wanted this togetherness, whatever it was called, to last forever.

Even in the crowded coffee shop the feeling of being alone together persisted. They laughed, talked or were companionably silent. And Cindy had never been so completely happy in her life.

"Surprise! Surprise!" Cindy heard a voice behind her cry. She saw the delight in Clay's eyes as he stood up.

"Clarice! I didn't know you guys were coming. This is great. Cindy, this is my sister, Clarice Edwards, and her husband, George."

Cindy felt as if she was surrounded by a crowd even though there were only three people—Clarice, George and a slender dark-haired woman named Julie Compton. Clay requested a table large enough to accommodate all of them, and this was arranged with surprising promptness. As they seated themselves around it, Cindy found herself wedged between Clarice and George. Clay sat across from her, having been captured by Clarice on one side and the dark-haired Julie on the other. Both women pressed this advantage and monopolized his attention.

"I wouldn't have missed this for anything," Clarice was saying. "When I heard what a great occasion it was going to be, my big brother getting the key to the city and everything, I told George to call Lisa for invitations."

Call Lisa? Oh, yes, Cindy reminded herself, Lisa Daniels's cousin was the one sponsoring the celebratory event. Cindy had almost forgotten, because so far there had been no sign of Lisa.

"I made Julie come because I knew you'd be glad to see her," Clarice chirped.

"I hope you don't mind." Julie had a soft lisp that somehow added to her youthful appeal. "I've been looking forward to seeing you again, Clay. It's been a while since I saw you last—Clarice's barbecue, I guess."

Cindy missed Clay's reply as she turned to answer George, who wanted to know if she was the acquisition analyst Clay had raved about. She said yes, she was, and that she was glad Clay was pleased. With an ear cocked for tidbits from across the table, she politely asked George where he worked. She was surprised to learn that for the past five years, he'd been the Northeast director of the Forest Paint Stores chain and also sat on Kencade Enterprises' board of directors.

"So it was easy for me to wangle an invitation to this shindig," he said. He told her they lived on Long Island and had two teenage sons.

Cindy managed to converse with George, though her attention was riveted on the others, who kept throwing out phrases that disconcerted her. "Clay, do you remember when...?" "We'll have to do that again." "Remember the last time you..." Cindy realized with a pang how little she really knew about Clay. He had a whole other life she hadn't even known about. True, Clay had mentioned his stepsisters, but Cindy hadn't given them much thought, had never actually considered the family history Clay shared with Clarice. Clarice, who was obviously quite determined to match up her brother with this Julie. Cindy began to feel quite isolated. And then—

"Oh, here you are, darling! When you weren't at the plant or in your room, I thought I might find you down here." Lisa Daniels appeared behind Clay's chair and slipped her slender white hands possessively onto his shoulders, massaging them so that her bracelets jangled as she greeted the others. "Hello, everybody. And Clarice—how nice to see you. I was so glad when George told me you were coming. This is a really big thing for Denver. And this affair tonight... I've been so busy, all this week."

All this week? She's been here... with Clay, thought Cindy, watching Lisa's hands sensuously caressing Clay through his thin cotton shirt.

The hands were forced to drop away as Clay stood up. "Hi, Lisa. I didn't know you were back. You know Clarice, George and Cindy, of course." He introduced Julie.

Lisa flashed them a brilliant smile. "Hello. So nice to meet you. I'm glad you're all here. I hope you'll excuse me, but I simply must drag this gorgeous man away. Honestly, I leave you alone for two days and everything goes haywire. I had to fly to New York for that charity ball committee meeting," she explained to the others before turning back to Clay. "You didn't even remember that you were supposed to meet with Leon Chambers this morning. He's going to be master of ceremonies, you know. He's waiting in my suite, so we'd better hurry. Excuse us, folks. See you all tonight."

It didn't matter to Cindy that Clay touched her arm and whispered, "Later," as Lisa led him away. What mattered was Lisa's hand still possessively on Clay's arm and the intimate way she looked up at him. What mattered was that she'd been here with him all week. *The only reason he had time for me yesterday was because she was away.* And she'd thought—

"That woman's a conniving witch!" said Clarice, her round face suffused with anger. "They've been busy all week," she mocked. "How much arranging does it take for a simple party!"

The same thought had crossed Cindy's mind.

"It's not a simple party," George said. "This is a big thing, Clarice. The Secretary of Labor is coming out from Washington."

"So?" Clarice retorted. "What's that got to do with Clay being dragged off by Lisa? And why does he have to confer with the master of ceremonies if she's giving the party?"

George shook his head and left, announcing that he was going for a swim.

"Oh, dear." Julie Compton's dark eyes looked bereft. "Perhaps I shouldn't have come. Clay's going to be so busy."

"Now, Julie, don't start that. Just wait until he sees you in that new ball gown. And don't worry about Lisa Daniels. She's been after him for two years and she hasn't got him yet."

"She's so beautiful," Julie said with a sigh.

"No prettier than you," Clarice decided. "And take that frightened look off your face. You look like one of your kindergarten kids on the first day of school."

"You're a schoolteacher?" Cindy asked, thinking of a conversation she'd once had with Maggie.

"Yes." Julie nodded and both women looked at Cindy as if they'd just noticed she was there.

"How...how nice," said Cindy, hearing Maggie's voice. *I thought for a while he was interested in this schoolteacher that one of his stepsisters was pushing. She's a rather attractive little thing.*

Yes, Julie was pretty. And Clarice, clearly a manipulative sister, was trying to force her on Clay. Then there was the beautiful Lisa, who didn't need anyone to plead her case or do any manipulating on her behalf. And Ms Denise Salter. And any number of other women. All of them clutching at Clay. Grasping and greedy.

And I'm one of them!

No! I'm darned if I'll go safariing with these huntresses!

Cindy felt as if she were suffocating. She couldn't wait to get out of the coffee shop.

"I must go. So good to have met you. I—I'll see you tonight." But she knew she wouldn't. She would not be a part of this. She would not play this "who's gonna catch him" game!

She went upstairs and packed. There was a plane leaving for Phoenix within two hours. She left a note in Clay's box and caught the shuttle to the airport.

CLAY MOVED through the hotel lobby searching for Cindy. He'd phoned her room from Lisa's suite but there was no answer. Surely she couldn't still be in the coffee shop. The swimming pool?

Lisa trailed behind him, arguing loudly. "Really, Clay, you're being quite impossible about this. The head table is already overcrowded and Ms Rogers simply has no official function whatsoever. Why does she have to be seated there?"

"Because I want her there."

"But how will she be introduced? It's not like she's your wife or anything."

He turned to face Lisa. "Not yet. But—" He stopped, seeing the stunned expression on her face. And something between anger and sadness smoldering in her green eyes. "Lisa, we've always been good friends, but..." There had been nothing else. Ever. He'd tried to cheer her up after her divorce. She was so unhappy then—in fact, he didn't think she'd completely recovered yet. But she always had something interesting and entertaining to do and often invited him to participate. He liked Lisa. She was kind and thoughtful. Tonight's party, for instance, had been entirely her idea. He didn't want...hadn't meant to hurt her.

"Lisa," he said softly, "I hope you haven't misunderstood. I never..." How could he say it? How could he explain what he only dimly understood himself? That Cindy had become the center of his universe and there was room for no other woman. "Lisa, I—"

She put a finger to his lips to silence him. "Don't say it. I understand. I may not like it, but...I do understand. Be happy, my friend." She blinked and gave his hand a slight pat before turning to walk toward the elevator.

He sighed, then started toward the swimming pool. A hotel clerk called to him. "Mr. Kencade. A message for you."

The clerk handed him the note and he stood there in the lobby reading it.

Clay,
Please forgive my rushing away like this. I had to leave for Phoenix. Enjoy your party. I'll be back in the office on Thursday.

Cindy

Had to leave. No explanation. As if he had nothing to do with it. No fond farewell. Just "back on Thursday." Strictly business.

Not exactly a slap in the face. But it sure as hell felt like one.

CHAPTER THIRTEEN

IT WAS GOOD TO BE with her parents again. Cindy hadn't seen them since last Christmas, when they'd flown east to spend the holidays with her and the children. Cindy noticed immediately that her mother's health was much improved, though she still walked with a cane.

"I do believe this sun has healing rays," said Angela Rogers, an older but still beautiful version of Cindy herself. She wasn't as sprightly as she used to be, Cindy reflected, but she'd lost none of the cheerfulness that had always been second nature to her.

The cheerfulness was reflected in the sunny two-bedroom apartment with its bright colorful cushions and draperies, the potted plants and the scattered books and magazines.

"You seem comfortable here," Cindy said.

"And busy," added Albert Rogers, her father. "You wouldn't believe the number of activities that go on in this so-called retirement complex. Your mother has become quite the social butterfly."

"And your father fancies himself quite the champion golfer," Angela chuckled. "At least, he's out on the course every morning trying to prove it."

As soon as she was settled Cindy called the Atwoods to let them know where she was. First, she allowed her parents to greet the Atwoods and talk to the children. When it was her turn, Johnny came on the line, and she had to blink away tears when she heard his voice. She missed the kids so much!

"Hi, Cindy." He sounded exuberant. "Guess what? In just two days we're leaving on our trip. And Grandpa says..." His voice rose high in a series of "grandpa says," ending with "He's a real neat guy. First we're going to Niagara Falls and then to Canada. Canada is a whole 'nother country, Cindy."

"It sounds like you're having a grand time," she said.

"Yeah. Wanna talk to Jamey? Jamey, here's Cindy."

Jamey talked excitedly about going to Canada, which, he too informed her, was another country "with a different flag and everything."

Then Cindy talked with Teri, who said that Grandma had given her a doll and promised she could take it with her on the trip.

Finally Mrs. Atwood got on the phone to say that they were enjoying the children so much, and that she was glad Cindy was having a vacation. "Don't worry about the kids," she reassured. "Just have yourself a good time. You certainly deserve it."

It *had* been a good time. A wonderful, fantastic, unbelievable time. That whole day with Clay, just the two of them. She'd thought that day was the beginning of forever.

The phone in her hand began to buzz. Startled, she replaced the receiver in its cradle. But she didn't move from the chair.

Yes, forever had entered her mind. The way Clay had looked at her, held her, kissed her... She'd felt so close to him that morning. Then the others had come. Cindy was staring at her mother's little telephone pad, but she was seeing Lisa's hands caressing Clay. She saw the schoolteacher's eager face as Clarice exclaimed, "Just wait until he sees you in that new ball gown." All such schemers!

Talk about the pot calling the kettle black. You *bought a new gown!*

Cindy bit her lip, thinking of the luscious turquoise dress that had cost more than she could afford. It had looked so simple on the hanger, but "like a dream on you," the clerk had said.

And you bought it to entice Clay! Just like Julie.

No. That's not true. I've been trying to push him away.

That was before you realized how special he is.

But I haven't been scheming!

No? How about this? "I could have Marcy and Steve and the children over one Sunday. And Clay." Like two families getting together with their children, she'd fantasized.

She bent her head in shame. Yes, she had even been thinking of using the children.

"Cindy, honey," Angela called. "Come on. Everything's ready."

She joined her parents in the breakfast nook, where her mother had set out a light supper of chicken salad, rolls and iced tea.

"How nice," she said, forcing all thoughts of Clay out of her mind, just as she had during the plane ride to Phoenix. She talked about the children, how happy they seemed with their grandparents. "I think I misjudged the Atwoods," she admitted.

"We all did," said her mother. "They have their problems, I guess, just as I have, crippled with this arthritis. And truly, Cindy, I think Claire would rather the children were with you."

"Maybe," Cindy said slowly, her fork poised over her salad. "I know I love having them. I can hardly wait for them to get back." She laughed. "Guess I can't stand the peace and quiet."

They talked about Jerry, her brother, who was now studying for the bar and already working in a commercial law firm. And thinking of getting married.

"His fiancée seems very nice," said Angela. "We talked to her on the phone."

Jerry, thought Cindy, two years younger than she. Getting married.

"And what about you, Cindy?" Albert asked. "You like the new job?"

"I like the pay. And, yes, I do like the job. You know..." She hadn't meant to talk about Clay. But when she started she couldn't seem to stop. She was unaware of the pride that glowed in her face as she began to describe his business ventures. "He takes over a business that's about to bomb out and—"

"Oh! One of those takeover guys, is he?" Her father almost slammed his glass down on the table.

"Now, Albert, don't go off on one of your rampages." Angela Rogers laid a restraining hand on her husband's arm. "Let Cindy tell us about—"

"But these conglomerates burn me up," he said. "They're taking over all the small businesses just so they can monopolize and control the economy."

Cindy, indignant, put down her fork. "Clay isn't like that. His takeovers are more like giveaways."

"Oh? So tell me."

Goaded by the skepticism in her father's voice, Cindy leaped to Clay's defense. "He never takes over. He just joins. Forming partnerships or corporations and showing people how to make a profit out of the mess they've created." She rapidly recited a list of examples. "*He's* the one who takes the risk. You don't know how hard I have to work to keep him from buying himself into bankruptcy—trying to save every broken-down business in the country."

"Cindy," cautioned her mother. "Calm down and eat your supper."

Cindy did manage to compose herself and enjoy the delicious salad. But she didn't stop talking. By the time Angela served ice cream, Albert Rogers threw up his hands and laughingly conceded.

"I surrender, Cindy. Your Clay Kencade is a knight in shining armor. No ice cream for me, dear," he added, turning to address his wife. "I'm going over to the clubhouse to shoot a little pool." On the way out he paused to rumple Cindy's hair. "Sounds like a rather responsible job, honey. I'm glad you're enjoying it."

"Mr. Kencade seems a very nice man," said Angela when they were alone.

"He is. And he's kind." Cindy told her how he had helped the children—the baseball practice and swimming lessons.

"My, my, he is nice. Spending so much time with them when he must be so busy." Angela dipped her spoon in her ice cream and gave her daughter a sidelong look. "Is he married?"

"Not yet. But there are plenty of people working on it."

"Oh? What do you mean?"

Cindy's temper flared again as she told her mother about the many women who frequented Clay's office. And about the machinations of Lisa and Julie in Denver. She did not tell her about Cindy Rogers and the trip to Red Rock.

"Oh, a womanizer." Her mother looked disappointed.

"Not really." Again Cindy felt compelled to defend Clay. "Although the tabloids have hung that reputation on him. He's just . . . well, kind, I guess, is the only word. Especially to women," she added, remembering Maggie's words. "He fancies himself a great protector."

"Humph! Sounds like he's the one who needs protecting—with all those women after him." Angela got up to stack the dishes, waving Cindy back. "No, I like to do this myself. Just sit there and talk to me. Now—are you?"

"Am I what?"

"After him?"

Cindy felt her face grow hot. "Of course not."

"Why not?"

"Mom!"

"Well, it's obvious you're crazy about him. I've never heard you talk so much about a man before. Not even that Dan fellow you were going to marry."

"Well, it's not because I . . . that is, I don't . . ." But she couldn't say it. She could not deny that she loved him. "You're not there, Mom. You don't know what it's like! All those women," she burst out.

"Does that surprise you? He sounds like a man any woman might be happy to marry."

"Yes, I suppose he is," Cindy agreed, thinking of Clay's patience with the children. Thinking of the tenderness of his kisses. She wished—

"Do you love him, Cindy?" Angela sat down to face Cindy.

"I . . . oh, yes," Cindy muttered as, to her horror, she felt the tears pouring down her cheeks. "Oh, Mom, I do! I've never felt this way about any other man. But I won't go shoving and pushing and—"

"He sounds like a man worth fighting for. What's wrong with a little competition?"

"You make it sound like a game!"

"One you have to play all your life," her mother said gently.

"No." Cindy angrily brushed away her tears. "If he really loved me he wouldn't have time for anyone else. He'd—"

"Kind men are vulnerable, honey. I know. I'm married to one of them."

Cindy looked at her mother and remembered a similar remark of Maggie's. *Clay is so vulnerable, especially where helpless women are concerned.* "But, Mom," she said defiantly. "I don't have time to go chasing after a man. I have my work and the children and—"

"That's another thing, Cindy." Her mother played absently with a fork. "The children. I'm glad you took them, because there was no one else to do it. But I worried then, and I worry now. I didn't want you to let them consume your whole life. It really bothered me when you broke up with Dan."

"I'm glad we broke up, Mom. I know now that I never really loved him."

"And you do love this man—Clay Kencade?"

"Yes, but I—"

Angela held up one hand. "Listen. I'm going to say something I've never said before. Your sister...she and John were very much in love when they married. But—I loved Claire, you know that. But when the children came... I even spoke to her about this and I'm not going to say it was all her fault, but she did seem to turn all her attention to the children. And John...well, you know what happened."

Cindy nodded. Poor Claire. She thought about Marcy and Steve—their love for each other seemed to blossom more fully with each of the children.

"Men need nurturing, too. Sometimes as much as children do."

"Yes."

"And sometimes they need protecting. Just like us." Angela tapped the table with her finger. "Some of these women you talk about may care more for Clay's money than for him."

Cindy drew a quick breath. Maggie's words almost exactly.

"It seems to me that you've been pretty diligent in protecting him in business. Why not in love? And, honey—" her mother touched her hand "—it's not really a fight. Just make his time with you happier than the time he spends with anyone else."

"*OH, OH,*" Maggie muttered as she caught sight of Clay's grim face on Monday morning. *Things did not go well.*

"Good morning, Mr. K.," she said brightly. "And how was the big party?"

"Great. Lots of perks. You'd think we saved Denver."

"A lot of bigwigs there?"

"Everyone that counted. Except Cindy," he said, giving her a rueful look. "Thanks, anyway. But it appears that she had to rush off to Phoenix for some unexplained reason."

"Hmm," said Maggie. "I must have overestimated your powers of, er, shall we say persuasion."

"I don't understand her." He shook his head, his expression blank. "I got tied up, Maggie. You know how it is, with everyone piling in…. Oh, yes, Clarice came with her husband and that friend of hers. And Lisa was there. Anyway, I turn my back for one minute and Cindy disappears. Leaving nothing but a note." He walked to the window and gazed out, juggling his keys in his pocket.

"Damn it! I just don't understand her." Clay turned back from the window, his bleak look changing to anger. "We were so close. I was going to suggest accompanying her to Phoenix, but… Hell, one minute we're close and the next she's cold as ice."

"Maybe you're so used to people who plunge right in that you can't understand those who test the water first," Maggie suggested softly.

"Yeah, and while she's testing the water," Clay said dispiritedly, "I'm in over my head!"

WHEN CINDY REACHED the office on Thursday morning, her mother's words still rang in her ears. "Business is your livelihood, honey, but love is your life. If you're lucky enough to find it, give it your all."

Fortified with her mother's advice, Cindy prepared to do just that. She did love Clay. It was a relief to admit it, freely and wholeheartedly, with no reservations. She loved everything about him—that lazy crooked smile, the way he cared about everyone... Johnny and Jamey. And her... She shut her eyes, remembering the trip to Red Rock. The way he had kissed her. Did that mean he loved her?

That's it, isn't it? You're scared. He's so rich, so handsome, so sought after. He might... break your heart? Desert the children?

"There's no life without risk, Cindy," her mother had said.

True. Those moments with Clay had been fuller than any others in her life. She would cherish them, no matter what. Had they been that way for him? Could she make him happy? Happier than anyone else?

She thought of Julie. Of Lisa. And Denise. *Don't think of other women,* she admonished herself. *Think of him!*

Oh, Clay, do you—could you love me? She wanted to see him, wanted to read the answer in those dark eyes. She wanted to touch him, show him....

Clay wasn't in the office.

"He had a couple of meetings this morning. And a luncheon. He probably won't be in till late," Maggie told her. "Anything important?"

"I just wanted to ask about this bid. It can wait." But *she* couldn't. She was aching to see Clay, to hear his voice.

"And did you enjoy your little vacation, Cindy?"

"Oh, yes, thank you," she said, recalling that it was Maggie who had made it possible. She began to tell Maggie how much she'd enjoyed the visit, how well her mother was doing.

"But you missed out on the big party." Maggie was fiddling with some papers on her desk and didn't look up. But there was something in her voice that sounded like a reprimand.

"The time was so short," Cindy said. "I thought I should spend it with my parents."

"I see," Maggie murmured. "First things first."

"Yes." And Cindy fled, wondering why Maggie's look made her feel so guilty.

Late in the afternoon, she was back in Maggie's office. "Any word from Clay?"

It was Tom who answered. He came in looking tired, frazzled and a little exasperated.

"Clay's at the site," he said, stooping to brush tobacco flakes from his pants. "I think he wants to take his dad's building down carefully, piece by piece, before they bring the wrecking ball in." He took his pipe from his pocket and shook it at them. "That boy's got too much sentiment."

"Well, you don't look very happy yourself," Maggie said briskly. "What's your problem? And don't empty that pipe into my wastebasket!"

Tom, arrested in this action, put his pipe back in his pocket and grunted, "Women!"

Cindy laughed. "Oh, Tom, I thought you liked us."

"Oh, I do. And you're quite welcome to your fresh unpolluted air. And all your rights, too. But I'll tell you one thing. It takes a hell of a lot more than the ERA to turn a hairdresser into a demolition expert."

"Oh, I see," said Maggie. "Denise Salter."

"You got it. She doesn't know a jackhammer from a pogo stick. But she's prancing around in that hard hat and those hobnail boots doing nothing but getting in the way." He strode out of the office muttering, "Women!"

"Men!" echoed Maggie, giving Cindy a significant look. "What does she need with a jackhammer? It's not the building she'd like to see fall!"

I'm not doing this because of what Maggie said, Cindy told herself a few minutes later as she climbed into a cab and headed for the demolition site. *He may not be in tomorrow and I need his signature on this bid so I can get it out. There's a deadline.*

But she knew she was speeding toward the site because she wanted to see him—and it had nothing to do with business.

The whole area was a shambles. A few apartment houses and office buildings were still intact, but most had been reduced to dusty piles of bricks and mortar. The workday was over and, except for a few crew members who were late in departing, the place was virtually deserted.

The cabdriver looked at the desolate area, then turned a puzzled face to her. "You sure this is where you want to go, lady?"

"Yes," Cindy said, looking at the five-story building in the southwest corner, still virtually untouched. His father's building, she thought. That was where he would be. If he was still there.

She paid her fare and got out. She skirted wrecking machinery and picked her way through piles of rubble toward the entry of the building. She hugged her briefcase to her chest, feeling a little ridiculous. It wasn't really necessary to track Clay down this way. After months of running away, she was now running after him. But she couldn't help it. She couldn't wait to see him—couldn't wait even one more day.

She saw two men place a heavy padded object in a big truck parked out front. When they reentered the building, she ran after them, intending to ask where she could find Mr. Kencade. Once inside, Cindy blinked to accustom herself to the dimness and heard Denise's voice, sounding loud and hollow in the empty building.

"Okay, that's it for tonight, guys. There are still some light fixtures Mr. Kencade wants to preserve. We'll start on those tomorrow. Make sure the truck is locked before you leave."

The men went out and Cindy called to Denise. "Pardon me, Ms Salter. Is Mr. Kencade still here?"

Denise turned and Cindy saw, with a prickle of dismay, that the construction overalls and hard hat only made Denise look frail and more helpless and yes, prettier than ever.

Denise frowned. "I'm not sure where Mr. Kencade is now. But Ms Rogers, this is a restricted area, you know. That means it's dangerous." Her condescending tone made Cindy grit her teeth. "You shouldn't be in here. Could I give Clay... Mr. Kencade a message for you?"

"No. I have some papers for him to sign."

"Oh, then give them to me," Denise said decisively. "I'll see that he gets them."

Cindy was feeling more than a little annoyed, but she managed to say calmly, "I'm sorry. These are rather personal and I'd better—"

"Then give them to me and I'll personally see that he personally gets them," Denise said with a sneer in her voice. "I don't think Mr. Kencade would appreciate your interference just now. You see he's got something he needs to discuss with me."

"You mean about which light fixtures he wants removed?" Cindy almost laughed. "Oh, for goodness' sake, get out of the way. I'll find him myself!"

Denise stepped in front of her. "Just a minute. I'd advise you to be careful how you speak to me—if you're interested in keeping your job."

"My job?" Cindy asked, genuinely puzzled.

"One never knows who might have influence," Denise said airily. "For your information, the discussion with Mr. Kencade involves far more than light fixtures. It has to do with a major business decision!"

"A business decision?" Cindy repeated, too stunned to say more.

"Oh, yes. It might surprise you to learn," Denise said, carefully removing her hat and shaking out her hair, "that Salter Demolition is considering a merger with Kencade Enterprises!"

A merger! The gall of the woman! Cindy felt like laughing again but managed to check it.

"No, Ms Salter," she said. "That doesn't surprise me in the least. Every sorry business in this country would like to merge, as you put it, with Kencade Enterprises!"

"Oh? Well I think you'd be surprised—and somewhat concerned, I gather—to hear that Mr. Kencade is quite open to joining with Salter Demolition!"

"No. That wouldn't surprise me, either. I'm already well aware of Mr. Kencade's efforts to keep your company alive and your men working. That's quite in line with his policies. And my concern is that you seem to be confusing his motives with a personal regard for yourself!" Ignoring Denise's attempts to interrupt her, Cindy spoke more rapidly. "My concern is that Mr. Kencade is too kind to tell you to take your sticky little hands back to hairdressing and leave the management of your demolition company to someone who knows a jackhammer from a pogo stick!''

A cough—or was it a chuckle?—sounded behind them, and both women turned to see Clay standing nearby.

Oh, Lord! How long had he been there? How much had he heard?

Denisc quickly began to speak in an altered and more appealing voice. ''Oh, Mr. Kencade, I've been looking for you. I wanted to ask—''

''Not now, Denise.'' He was looking at Cindy, an expression on his face that she couldn't define. ''You wanted to see me, Cindy?''

''Just some papers for you to sign. You can do it later, if you're busy,'' she said. And fled, thoroughly ashamed. They'd been fighting over him like two magpies over a bauble. And he had heard!

''Cindy! Wait!''

She didn't listen. Running, stumbling, she made her way through the rubble.

''Hey,'' he called. ''You're going in the wrong direction.''

She didn't care. She just wanted to get away. Her heel sank into a crack and she would have fallen had he not caught her. He turned her to face him.

''Cindy, you're jealous!''

''I am not!'' She jerked away and ran blindly on.

''You are. And that's why you left me in Denver,'' he shouted, as he pursued her. ''Look, I promise—oh, damn!''

Hearing a string of curses and realizing that he had fallen, Cindy whirled and ran back to him.

''Oh, Clay!'' she cried. ''Are you hurt?'' He was sitting up, examining his torn pant leg. ''Oh, I'm sorry. Let me see. Are you hurt?''

He looked up at her and scowled, "Give me the damn papers you want me to sign!"

"Oh, never mind those. Let's see if—"

"Give me the papers!" He sounded so ferocious that she handed them to him. But she knelt beside him, a worried expression on her face. "Oh, let me see," she said, pulling the torn fabric aside to examine his leg.

"Never mind that! Let's just get this cleared up," he said, thrusting the papers back into her hand. "Here!"

She looked down to see scrawled in big letters: *I love you, Cindy Rogers. Will you marry me?*

"Oh!" She sank back on her heels, unmindful of the broken bricks that poked her, unmindful of the dust and debris. She looked down at the words he had written, hardly daring to believe. "Oh, Clay, are you sure? Do you mean—"

"For Pete's sake, Cindy, don't give me the 'this is so sudden' bit. We've been through accusations of harassment and the whole 'strictly business' routine. Now, there it is—my honorable intentions in writing!" He jabbed a finger toward the paper. "Just answer the damn question!"

"Oh, Clay! Yes. Oh, yes!" She flung her arms around him and covered his face with kisses. "Oh, yes, Clay. Yes. Yes. I love you! I love you so much!"

"Well, now," Clay said, laughing as he took her in his arms, "I'd have put my intentions in writing a long time ago, if I'd known you were going to be so grateful!"

"Oh, don't be smug!" she said. But she didn't care. She felt smug, too. She nestled against him, not wanting to move. Savoring the moment, the knowledge that this man, this wonderful man, was hers—to hold and to cherish. To share happiness with and— She sat up. "Clay. The children. I know you love them but . . .'' She gave him a tentative smile. "Every day . . . forever? Are you sure you—"

"I ought to know what kind of stepfather to be! I've had lots of experience with step-families. Now give me your answer in writing. Sign right here," he said, pointing to his lips.

Cindy happily complied.

HARLEQUIN
Romance

Coming Next Month

#3067 ANOTHER MAN'S RING Angela Carson
Judi knows she doesn't want to marry Robert—but breaking it off won't be easy. A job offer in Thailand provides an escape, until she realizes that working for Nick Compton, she's jumped from the frying pan into the fire!

#3068 LOVE'S RANSOM Dana James
Zanthi enjoys her diplomatic post as assistant secretary on a small Caribbean island—but she senses something very odd is happening. Especially when surveyor Garran Crossley arrives and she is assigned to accompany him on his land survey....

#3069 THE TURQUOISE HEART Ellen James
Annie Brooke travels to New Mexico to restore a damaged painting for Derek Richards. A simple job, she thinks. But the feelings Derek arouses in Annie's heart are far from simple....

#3070 A MATTER OF PRINCIPAL Leigh Michaels
Patrick's job is to sort out Camryn's finances—but he is threatening her whole way of life. To protect herself and her young daughter, Camryn has to fight him, though he proves difficult to resist—both as a banker and as a man!

#3071 HILLTOP TRYST Betty Neels
Oliver Latimer is safe and reassuring, and Beatrice is glad he was there to pick up the pieces when her life turned upside down. Against Colin Ward's charm, however, Oliver seems to have nothing to offer—until Beatrice takes a good second look....

#3072 A SUMMER KIND OF LOVE Shannon Waverly
Recently widowed, Joanna Ingalls needs a quiet summer alone with her five-year-old son. But when they arrive at her father's cottage, she's shocked to find Michael Malone living there—the man she'd loved so desperately six years before.

Available in August wherever paperback books are sold, or through Harlequin Reader Service:

In the U.S.
901 Fuhrmann Blvd.
P.O. Box 1397
Buffalo, N.Y. 14240-1397

In Canada
P.O. Box 603
Fort Erie, Ontario
L2A 5X3

You'll flip . . . your pages won't!
Read paperbacks *hands-free* with

Book Mate • I

The perfect "mate" for all your romance paperbacks

Traveling • Vacationing • At Work • In Bed • Studying • Cooking • Eating

Perfect size for all standard paperbacks, this wonderful invention makes reading a pure pleasure! Ingenious design holds paperback books OPEN and FLAT so even wind can't ruffle pages — leaves your hands free to do other things. Reinforced, wipe-clean vinyl-covered holder flexes to let you turn pages without undoing the strap . . . supports paperbacks so well, they have the strength of hardcovers!

Pages turn WITHOUT opening the strap

SEE-THROUGH STRAP

Reinforced back stays flat

Built in bookmark

BOOK MARK

BACK COVER HOLDING STRIP

10 x 7¼ . opened
Snaps closed for easy carrying. too